Yard Sale of the Undead

My Life Among the Undead:
Book 2

Camara M. Bragdon

DEDICATION

This book is dedicated to my nieces: Kierra, Esther, Lydia, Abby, Elisabeth, and Isabelle: The first members of my fan club.

My Life Among the Undead books

Friend of the Undead

CHAPTERS

1. Oh, the Things You Will Find at Yard Sales

2. Dad Makes an Executive Decision about Karaoke

3. Eddie Falls Off My Ceiling

4. It Can't Be Killed, Captain!

5. My Wish is Granted, Sort of.

6. I Make an Unpleasant Discovery at My House.

7. Why Dirk Should Never be an Exterminator

8. When a Spider Is Not Really a Spider

9. She's Gone Mad! Stark Raving Mad!

10. Why Tragedy Songs Aren't Good Choices for Karaok

Prologue: Five Years Ago

My name is Michelle Anderson, "Shelly" to my friends, and this is how I entered a magical world.

Pembrook used to be a quiet, safe town in New England with a population of 1,500 where everybody knows everybody's business. My dad, Timothy Anderson, wanted to raise my older brother, Robin, and me someplace with a low crime rate, but that all changed the summer after I graduated from college.

Matthew Harris, the well-respected chief of police, had retired after thirty years on the police force and was replaced by Thomas Mallory, a man with the face of a weasel. My dad hated working under the new chief who made sure that every officer on the force worked twelve-hour shifts, but because he was a widower, he felt that he had no choice. "It's my job, and I have to do it whether I like it or not!" he would tell Robin and me. The officers' salaries slowly began decreasing without any explanation. Dad confronted Mallory on several occasions, but the chief would constantly deny any knowledge of the decrease in pay. Even I tried to pitch in financially, but my measly paycheck from Wal-Mart couldn't even afford me an apartment, much less help Dad out.

"Look, Timothy," Mallory had told my father in a "best buddy" voice (Dad hated it when his supervisors tried to patronize him), "don't worry about your pay. It's probably all in your head."

Then there was the case Dad was working on. He and his team had been trying to crack down on a large heroin ring that had filtered into Pembrook, and he suspected that the new chief was somehow involved. When Dad caught me eavesdropping while he was discussing the case with his friends, he looked at me and said, "Shelly, you should never listen in on people's conversations. You may not like what you discover."

Late one night I woke up to hear a heated argument coming from downstairs. Crawling out of bed, I went to the head of the stairs and listened as my dad argued with three of his coworkers.

"You can't go around accusing Mallory of heading up the drug ring, Timothy!" That was Detective Bruce Miller, my dad's partner, and best friend.

"Yeah, Bruce is right. We've got no evidence!" replied Andrew Baker, another detective on the force who had grown up with my father.

"Do you really want to lose your job if your theory is wrong?" Bruce snapped.

"I know I'm right!" Dad shouted, slamming his fist on the table. "What about last night's raid? His car was there, and he denied it! Why do you think I ran the plates? We have to confront Mallory. He'll never turn himself in."

A collective gasp came from Andrew and Bruce. "Are you crazy? You know the rumors about what happened in Littleton?"

"This is our duty, guys! When I took the oath twenty years ago, I meant it. Did you?"

There was a long silence, and then Bruce spoke. "I can't do this, Timothy. If I get fired, I don't know if I can get another job."

"Natalie and I can't live on her salary alone," Andrew replied. "I'm not willing to take that chance."

"You know Mallory's corrupt," Dad said. "First, the disappearances and then the sudden increase in drug-related crime. Why do you think he ordered us to close Matt's case less than a week after he disappeared? He said that there was no evidence of foul play. Which is complete bull! Mallory closing the case is what probably led to Chris' suicide."

I recognized the Texan drawl of Henry "Dusty" Williams voice as he spoke softly. "That and other things."

A moment of silence hung in the air. A loud sneeze overcame me, and I heard chairs being pushed back from the kitchen table. My cover was blown. I got up from my position, rushed into the bathroom, and flushed the toilet.

"Shelly?" Dad called from the bottom of the stairs.

"Yeah!" I replied as if I had just woken up. "What's going on?"

"Nothing! Bruce, Dusty and Andrew are just leaving." Dad's voice was very stern. "Go back to bed."

I did as I was told. As I lay in bed, I could hear the four detectives speaking in hushed tones as they went outside. I have never been psychic, but I had a bad feeling that things were going to get worse before they got better.

The next day I came home from my early morning shift at Wal-Mart and saw Dad's green Chevy Blazer sitting in the driveway. "That's odd. Dad's shift doesn't end until eight," I said to myself. I went inside to the kitchen and was about to raid the refrigerator when I heard something in the basement.

I cautiously opened the basement door and went down the stairs. Our basement had been recently cleaned after it had flooded last spring. Other than the laundry corner, the only other used part of the basement is Dad's home gym with a weight bench and a well-used punching bag. That was where I saw my tall, muscular father. He was wearing his work-out clothes, a tank top, and mesh shorts. He punched the bag hard, nearly knocking it off the rafters. "Those backstabbing maggots! They knew what Mallory was, and yet they said nothing!" he yelled at no one in particular. He did a spinning round kick at the punching bag causing one of the screws to dangerously loosen. I realized something had really angered him. Like my grandfather, Dad has a temper. Unlike my grandfather, Dad only lets his anger out on his punching bag.

"Dad, what's wrong?"

Dad stopped and saw me sitting on the steps. Tears were rolling down his cheeks. He sighed, clearly not wanting to tell me why he was so upset. "I lost my job!" he finally said.

I knew that Mallory fired my dad just because he stood up for what was right, and I admired Dad for that. I walked over to my father and threw my arms around him. "I'm so sorry, Dad!"

He put his arms around me. "It's all right, Shelly. We're going to be okay."

As if it weren't hard enough for Dad to lose his job, the death threats started. First, it was just harmless, mysterious letters. Then curse words were sprayed on our front door. Even

my dad's friends had turned against him, especially Bruce who

had told Dad that he was a pathetic liar for trying to frame

Mallory. He never believed that Mallory was part of the drug ring.

Finally, Dad decided to go to the press with the story, and

that's when the real threats started. All the tires on Dad's Chevy

Blazer were slashed one night. Someone bashed in the

windshield of the car and tossed a mysterious package in the

front seat. Fortunately, it didn't set off any detonators or a cloud

of anthrax. The worst was yet to come.

Late one night, I woke up to the smell of smoke.

Instinctively, I grabbed my purse and my photo album and raced

down the stairs. I gasped in horror as I saw the living room

curtains engulfed in flames. The big living room window had

been shattered from the outside. "Dad! Robin!" I managed to

scream in between coughing fits. Smoke filled my lungs and

stung my eyes as I strained to see where my family was.

The next thing I knew Dad grabbed my hand and pulled

me outside to where Robin was waiting in the passenger seat of the Blazer. We piled in and sped out of the driveway. I turned around watching the home that my dad had built with his own hands-the home I grew up in-engulfed in flames.

Dad drove for hours in complete silence. We didn't know where we were going. We just wanted to get away from Mallory and away from Pembrook. Everything changed for us. Now we were a family on the run.

I leaned my head against the window and closed my tired eyes. When I opened them a few minutes later, I saw a large pinkish, purplish ball of light swirling consistently, but it seemed to stay in one place and got larger and larger. It began to pull us toward it. Dad glanced up at me through the rearview mirror for a moment. "Hang on, guys!" he said to Robin and me in an incredibly calm voice. "We're going through!"

Chapter One:

Oh, the Things You Will Find at Yard Sales

Cricket Lunesta and I walked down Wildflower Street, a middle-class residential area in the city of Zephyr. It was eleven o'clock on a beautiful Saturday morning as the fairy and I turned into the driveway which was scattered with tables loaded with clothes from decades past, out-of-date medical and geographical books, and other odd accessories that you would only find at yard sales. I don't mind going to yard sales, but today I wasn't in the mood. In fact, I had been released from the hospital the week before. A few weeks ago I was attacked by a couple of gargoyles and had gotten in a motorcycle accident. My back was still healing, and I was so glad that this was our last stop. We had hit about a dozen other yard sales with no success. Actually,

the lack of success was on my part.

"So, when did you and Eddie become a couple?" Cricket

asked. Apparently, I hadn't heard the fairy. She flew on her pale

green, moth-like wings, landed softly in front of me, and looked

at me with her hazel eyes. "Earth to Shelly Anderson! Come in!"

I looked at the fairy. "I'm sorry, Cricket. What did you

say?"

She shook her head of honey-colored hair as her two

beige, feathered antennae flopped back and forth. "I said, 'When

did you and Eddie become a couple?' Or is that a rumor?"

I carefully bent down to look at a box full of books. "While I

was in the hospital."

"I knew that you two would make a cute couple," my

coworker said with a smile. "You're so perfect for each other."

She had walked to the table next to me and began sifting

through a box of baby clothes. She held up a little dress with

green smiling turtles on it. "Isn't this adorable?"

"Oh, that is so cute. It's going to look adorable when the baby's older." I looked at Cricket's round belly. This was Cricket's first baby, and she was very excited about becoming a mother. "Remind me again, when did you say you were due?"

"Mid-December!"

"Ah, a Christmas baby!" said a voice behind us.

We turned around to see an elderly werewolf dressed in a plaid shirt and jeans coming out from the garage that was attached to the modest pink and white ranch home. With the exception of his tufted ears, he looked like a normal human being. "My daughter, Mayberry, was a December child," he said to us. "Now, about this dress, I will sell it to you for two druci. Come," he said as he graciously took her hand, "I'll show you a hand-woven bassinet that I acquired from an elf queen in Pedestria."

I smiled as I went back to my browsing. There was no need to fear the old Were. Even in his wolf form, the old man was a kindly, sophisticated gentleman. In fact, he had retired from his job as Zephyr's ambassador about five years before and was moving into a smaller house with his daughter and five grandchildren.

If you're wondering how I knew all this, I'll let you in on a widely known fact among my family and friends. When a human, like me, leaves one reality through a time portal into another reality, such as the magical city-state of Zephyr, he or she gets some kind of magical ability. I've got an interesting power: limited telepathy. Meaning, I can read the minds of the undead and telecommunicate with them. Were people fall into the undead category because they turn to their animal form only at night.

Knowing that Cricket was going to be a long time, I decided to check out if the box of coffee table books had anything interesting. Two items caught my eye. The first was a deck of unopened cards with elaborate pictures on them. The top card showed an image of a man with a brightly colored bundle slung over his shoulder as he walked along a country road. There was an inscription on the bottom that read *ingress*. I glanced at the handwritten price tag. "One druci, not too bad," I said aloud.

The second item was a book. A huge picture of a furious-looking hurricane whipped across the cover of *Wild and Wacky Weather* by the famous storm chasing satyr, Luther Hornswaggle. I flipped through it, glancing at photographs of crumbled houses, fallen trees, and other proof of the destruction of natural disasters. It looked pretty cool. Since I am attracted to weird stuff, I decided to track down the werewolf and the fairy.

"How much for this book?" I asked Mr. Norton Wolfbane.

"One druci," he told me. He watched as I got the money out of my purse. "I have never seen anyone look at that book other than myself and the wizard who sold it to me."

"Well, I really like this type of stuff," I replied with a smile. After Cricket paid forty druci for the bassinet, several pieces of baby clothes, and a couple of bibs, we walked back to my house. Her husband, Max, was going to pick up the bassinet when he got out of work tonight.

"He seemed like a nice man," Cricket replied as she happily swung her bag full of clothes over her shoulder.

"Most of the undead are."

"Especially a certain vampire. Right, Shelly?"

I unlocked the door to my house, and Cricket and I stepped inside the kitchen. "Let's set our stuff on the table before we go to lunch and a movie," I said as I stepped on some water. Suddenly, my left foot slid forward as my right knee hit the floor with a loud, painful THUD. My book on disasters leaped out of my hands and skidded under the table. "Ow! That really hurt!"

"Are you okay? You fell pretty hard on your knee."

I grimaced as I touched my bruised knee. I was going to be in pain for the rest of the day. Squatting down, I picked up my purchase by the spine and shook it gently, making sure that nothing was wedged between the pages. A small rainbow-colored spider fell onto the linoleum. I tried to smack it with the palm of my free hand, but it scurried under the refrigerator. I was in too much pain to chase after it.

Cricket gave a short shriek. "What was that?" She jumped so high I thought she was going to have the baby right then and there.

"It's just a spider!" I assured her. The fairy's reaction to the arachnid reminded me of my childhood friend, Lisa Miller. Lisa would nearly go into cardiac arrest every time she saw one of those eight-legged creatures. I smiled to myself as we left my house for lunch at Murphy's and then a matinee movie.

I felt really bad about leaving Cricket at the movies, but my knee was turning unattractive shades of black and blue and hurt like heck. Cricket completely understood and told me that she would fly home after the movie and take a nap. The friendly cab driver dropped me off at my house, and I limped into the living room where I collapsed onto my couch. Remembering what my dad always told me whenever I bruised myself, I managed to get out of my comfortable position and limped into the bathroom where I found a cloth ice pack. After I filled it with water from the sink, I hobbled to the freezer and dropped some ice cubes into the ice pack. Fortunately, I had just cleaned my house, and I made it back to the couch without incident.

My photo album sat on the little end table with my lava lamp. That album had been through a lot in the past five years. I suddenly wanted to relive all those memories from long ago. As

I placed the ice pack on my swollen knee, I heard a knock on my door.

"Who is it?"

"It's your brother! I'm dropping off the movie I borrowed."

"Come on in!" I wasn't going to get up for my brother.

The door opened, and I heard Robin walk through my kitchen and into my living room. His deep blue eyes settled on the ice pack. "What did you do to yourself, Shelly? Or shall I call you 'Gimpy?'"

I rolled my eyes at him. "I fell! Okay!"

He tossed a DVD onto my lap. "Here's the movie I borrowed. It was interesting. I didn't realize you liked fly fishing."

I glanced at the title which read *Big Bill's Famous Fly Fishing Moments*. "I have never seen this movie in my life."

"Oh, crap! I think I borrowed it from one of the guys at the station." My brother has followed my dad's footsteps in law enforcement as a sergeant with the Zephyr police force. He has cropped brown hair and deep blue eyes, which in his mind cause the ladies to fawn over him on a daily basis. "I should've known that you would never buy a movie on fly fishing. Remember the time when Dad and Bruce took all of us fishing? That was a great time."

"All of us," referred to Dad's police partner, Bruce Miller and his twins, Lisa and Roger. "I remember that time. I got sick."

He smiled at me. "And puked while we were gutting the fish."

"It was disgusting." I shivered at the thought. "Fish guts were everywhere. You and Roger thought it was hysterical."

"Come on, Shelly. You really couldn't tell the difference between the vomit and the fish guts."

"Thank you for reminding me once again why I rarely eat fish." I opened up the photo album and flipped to a picture of me, my brother, and the Miller twins at the lake the summer before our ninth-grade year.

Robin looked at the picture. "This must have been taken after you threw up because you look a little green."

I ignored his snide remark. "Do you ever wonder what happened to Bruce, Roger, and Lisa?"

"Sometimes, but I'm sure they made out fine. I bet Lisa got her own home makeover show, and Roger's probably playing pro-football."

"Or she could be doing event-planning. She was always planning parties. You remember she planned the entire senior prom. But I agree with you about Roger. He's probably the quarterback for the Miami Dolphins." I began laughing as I recalled the time Roger tried to teach Robin football. "He's much better at the game than you are. I can still see your look of horror when the football sailed over across the street. The ball actually came within five inches of the front window of our next-door neighbor's house before it took out all of Mrs. Kingley's flowers in her window boxes."

"It's was a bad throw."

"Yeah, and Dad and Bruce made you and Roger replant everything the following Saturday."

"But at least I didn't have to repaint the window boxes."

"I still think Bruce was a little unfair to make Roger do all the painting."

Robin shrugged. "Bruce was a little strict, but his heart

was in the right place. Don't forget that when Mom died, Bruce

helped Dad deal with her death." My brother was right. Bruce

really knew what it was like to lose a spouse having lost his wife

to cancer when the twins were only ten.

I shook my head. "Unfortunately, Bruce wasn't there for

Dad when he got fired."

Robin nodded in agreement. "Glad that's in the past." We

were silent for a few minutes until he got up and grabbed his

video. "You coming to the diner tonight?"

I nodded.

"Of course, you are. Eddie's working tonight. See you

later." He walked out the door.

"Bye, Robin!" After we entered Zephyr, I had never seen

nor heard from the Millers again. I wondered how they were

doing, and I really wanted to see them again.

Unfortunately, the only possible way to see my friends

was to open up a wormhole in from one reality to another. My

boyfriend, Eddie, thinks that the portal to Zephyr only opens

when people from another reality are in desperate trouble. How it opens is unknown. For some strange reason, my boyfriend knows a lot about magic, more than he cares to tell me.

I closed the photo album and set it back on the stand. I smiled when I thought about Eddie. He is such a great guy and a hottie! I immediately dismissed the thought of calling him because he sleeps during the day. *I'll see him tonight at the diner*, I told myself. Actually, sleep sounded like a good idea.

"Help! Someone help us! Can anyone hear us? We need help!"

I find myself standing next to a tall brick wall. My ear is pressed against the wall. Lisa is banging on the other side with her fists and screaming. A gunshot rings out and then silence.

I woke up with a start, nearly falling off my couch and colliding with my oak coffee table. My heart was pounding hard, and I tried to remember where I was. The pain in my knee had subsided, but it was now sporting a pretty black and purple bruise. "What a weird dream!" I said aloud to myself. My stomach growled, and I checked my watch. Fifteen after six. I needed to get going. Quickly running a comb through my hair, I grabbed my

purse and went outside to the little stable where my brown and

white-winged horse, Jordan, was chomping on some hay and

oats. She's a gentle horse and waited patiently as I slowly

saddled up. "To Anderson's Place!" I told the horse as I climbed.

Winged horses are pretty cool. They can understand

human speech. All you need to do is tell them where you want to

go, and they will take you there. You can fly, and you don't even

need to worry about refueling every three hundred or so miles.

It's fun and great for the economy! Jordan began galloping out of

her stall. Once we had cleared the shed, she was up flying in

the cool night air. All the way over to the diner, I couldn't get the

odd dream out of my mind.

Chapter Two:

Dad Makes an Executive Decision about Karaoke Music

It was almost seven o'clock when Jordan and I landed in the back parking lot of my dad's diner. Tradewinds, the giant golden eagle that my dad owned, was preening himself to catch the attention of Amelia's giant white eagle, Scotia. I smiled. The birds were just as cute as my dad and his girlfriend. When the winged horse landed gently beside Eddie's motorcycle, she whined a bit as I painfully slid off her back. I shuffled slowly to the back entrance where I spotted two elfin waitresses in their forties taking a smoke break. Elves in Zephyr are not little green forest folk who live in trees and make shoes for a living. In fact, they are not much different from regular humans with the exception of their pointed ears. I waved to the girls as I walked up to them. "Hi, Mari, Cherry! Taking a break early?"

Cherry, the oldest of the two, nodded. "Mr. Anderson's trying to get some of that wiring fixed in the dining area," she replied as she blew out a puff of cigarette smoke. "So, the diner's been closed for an hour."

I nodded my thanks as I opened the heavy steel door and into the kitchen. A blast of warm air mixed with the smell of pork chops and my dad's famous sour cream apple pie hit me with full force. I wrapped my arms around myself as I gently walked across the freshly waxed kitchen floor. The last thing my aching body needed was an unexpected slide into one of the two ovens or the chest freezer on the other side of the kitchen. I was grateful that nobody was in the kitchen to ask me why I was limping.

I followed familiar voices into the main dining area where I saw Dad, Amelia, and Eddie looking up at the ceiling. Looking skyward, I saw a Winged One high above us in the peak of the dark wooden cathedral ceiling. Dad must have turned off the main lights so the Winged One wouldn't fry himself.

Angels. That's the one thing that comes close to describing these beautiful humanoids with their magnificent bird-like wings sprouting from their shoulder blades. Winged Ones are quite similar to humans, except their bones are hollow and strong as a bird's. When standing, a Winged One's wings barely touch the ground by only a few inches but are longer than two-arm spans on each side. The bones enable their wings to fly for many miles on end. I recognized this Winged One by his green and blue parrot wings. It was Tobian Avis, the self-employed window washer and newly certified electrician. He fiddled around with what looked like wires. "Okay, Timothy, hit the lights!" he yelled down to my father.

Dad, with his elasticity, stretched his arm all the way across to the other side of the room and clicked on the light switch. The bulb flickered a couple of times before there was a slight boom. Being the closest, Mr. Avis was, fortunately, wearing goggles to protect his eyes from the flying shards of glass and filament. He flew back down to the floor and folded his wings behind his back. "I'm sorry, Timothy," he said as he shook his head, "but you need someone who knows more about electricity than I do."

My dad ran his fingers through his short brown hair. I could have sworn that I saw some gray hairs. For the past few weeks, he'd been having trouble with the electricity in this old building which had been turned into a family-style diner. He pulled out his wallet and was about to write a check. "That's all right, Tobian, at least you did what you could."

"Don't bother, Timothy. I only expect payment when I actually repair something." The Winged One shook my dad's hand as Dad reluctantly put back his wallet. Mr. Avis picked up his toolbox off the floor and left the diner.

With her mind, Amelia moved the broom and dustpan from behind the ice cream counter where my boyfriend works. I gently stepped out of her way as she began sweeping up the glass. "Shelly, how long have you been here?" she asked.

"Long enough to see the glass bulb explode." I gingerly eased up onto one of the black leather stools at the ice cream counter.

The tall and dashing Eddie Van Helsing came around the counter. "Hey, Shelly," the vampire said as he put on his black apron. "How was your yard sale excursion?" he asked. His striking green eyes looked down at the bruise on my knee. "What happened to you?"

"I had a little accident earlier today."

Eddie shot me a fanged smile. "I had no idea that old ladies at those yard sales could be so vicious."

"Very funny!" I playfully stuck my tongue out at my boyfriend. He was wearing a pair of black jeans and a grass green collared shirt with the sleeves rolled up just above his elbows. Was it me or was he getting cuter every day? He had taken my advice to get his curly, jet black hair cut. "I'll have the usual!" Even though we had just started officially dating, I still couldn't bring myself to call Eddie any pet names just yet. It sounded weird.

The vampire bent down to get a glass. He went to the soda fountain and poured me a glass of cream soda. Then he put a spoonful of strawberry powder mix into the glass. It was my own special drink that he concocted just for me after we had become friends. Eddie stuck a straw in the glass and handed it to me.

I started to stir the straw round and round. The fizzy bubbles popped and formed repeatedly. The disturbing dream filled my mind as I tried desperately not to cry in front of the vampire.

Eddie saw the tears in my eyes. "Are you okay?" he asked. Who said vampires don't have souls? He came over, sat down on the stool next to me and handed me a napkin. "What's wrong, Shelly?"

"I'm fine," I said as I wiped my eyes with the hardest paper napkin in the world. But a napkin is a napkin, and I appreciated Eddie's concern. "I was just looking at some old pictures that brought back some pretty strong memories," I said. I told him everything, including the weird dream. Eddie knows a little bit about my life in Pembrook. "I just miss Lisa, that's all." I finally said as I handed my boyfriend the wet napkin.

"That's normal, Shelly. Everyone misses their childhood friends."

"I know, but Lisa and I were best friends. I wish that I could talk to her again. I mean, we would tell each other everything. We even had our future boyfriends planned at the age of ten." I smiled at the childish memories.

"Did your plans include a hot-looking vampire?"

"You know what I mean, Eddie. Before I came here, I didn't even know that vampires could be vegetarians, much less that you guys even existed." I wanted to forget my hurt and concentrate on the dream. "What are your thoughts on my dream?"

He shrugged. "I don't know what to make of it, Shelly. It could be related to the conversation that you had with Robin. You might be feeling afraid that you don't know what's going on in your friend's life, and you want to be a part of that."

"Ooh, Eddie Van Helsing: spy, bounty hunter, ice cream counter attendant, and shrink! How do you do it?"

The vampire shook his head. "Someone once told me that 'Dreams aren't just a weird mix of images that dance in and out of your brain. They are the messages in the fortune cookies of your mind.' Of course, the person who told me might have been a little wasted."

Another story for another time. "I'm serious, Eddie. I really think that Lisa and her family are in danger."

Eddie raised an eyebrow. "Really? In what kind of danger?"

I shrugged. "I don't know, but I just can't shake the feeling that she's in danger." I hesitated with the next question. "Can you open a wormhole?"

He shook his head. "I would really like to help you, but I can't open a wormhole."

"I thought you knew a lot of magic."

"Yes, but that's something that I'm not capable of." Eddie put his arm around me and gave me a much-needed hug. He hopped off the stool and went behind the counter. "I'd better get back to work before your dad yells at me. Like he has been lately."

"What? What do you mean?"

"After the incident with the Chairman, your father has been to grilling me on why I wasn't there for you, and he keeps calling me your 'guardian.'"

"'Guardian?' What's he talking about?"

The vampire shrugged. "I have no idea. Whenever I asked him about it, he changes the subject."

This was totally not like my father. "I'll talk to him." I managed to smile as I finally took a sip of soda. Eddie is the best boyfriend that a girl could have, and there was no way that I was going to lose him. He was kind, considerate, and his cuteness was definitely an added bonus. Lisa would have been so jealous of me, in a good kind of way. I heard the main doors open, and I had a silly thought that Lisa would be walking through the doors. I turned around as my dream was crushed when Robin and his best friend, Strider Hornsby, walked through the doors. "Hey, Eddie!" Robin called. "Have you seen my dad?"

The vampire nodded as he cleaned off the countertop. "Yeah, he's in the kitchen." He saw the small machine in Strider's hands. "That is not your karaoke machine, is it?"

The satyr came over to the bar and set the machine next to me on the counter. "Actually, this baby's a rental. Mine's a little bigger."

I looked over at Eddie who told me mentally that both Robin and Strider have been trying to convince my dad to have a karaoke night at the diner. "Oh, good, that's just what this respectable diner needs: a karaoke bar!"

"Shelly! I can't believe that you'd go against your own brother and his best friend!" Robin was shocked. "That's defamation of karaoke!"

Eddie snorted. "Karaoke has character?" He leaned across the counter and gave me a high five. "That's a new one."

Strider kicked his hoof into my sneaker. "Shelly, I don't think you're being fair to the legend of karaoke! Think of all the benefits that karaoke has brought into the world."

"And those would be what?"

There was a long silence as the satyr tried to count all of the contributions on his fingers. Unfortunately, he couldn't get past his thumb. He adjusted his gray rasta cap back on his two horns. "Well, there are a lot of them, but I just can't think of any right at the moment."

"Wait," Robin said, "I got one, Strider. It brought fun into bars."

Eddie shook his head. "Mr. Anderson doesn't serve alcohol here."

"He might start if a karaoke bar is put in here," I replied as I downed my soda. Eddie was about to ask if I wanted a refill, but I shook my head no.

"This place will be fun with a karaoke machine," Robin replied.

"I guess Billiards Night is not fun anymore," Eddie said. He really liked playing pool with Robin, Strider, and his brother, Dirk on Tuesday nights. Then an idea crossed his mind, and he looked at me. "You know what, Shelly, I read this study that said karaoke machines can cause brain damage."

"Really?" I said with an evil grin. "Then I guess it's not just the tone-deaf, disillusioned singers who are consuming large amounts of alcohol that causes it."

Dad came out into the dining room and took one look at the karaoke machine. "No, Strider! Absolutely not!" Before Strider or Robin could open their mouths in protest, he cut them off. "I will not have a karaoke machine installed in my diner. They only cause trouble."

By causing the eardrums to bleed when someone sings off-key, Eddie subliminally told me. I had to grab a napkin to conceal my laughter as the vampire joined in. The others looked at us as if we were sharing a private joke.

Dad ignored Eddie and me. "My answer is still no, Strider. I have bad memories of karaoke when I used to be a cop."

"Like what?" Robin asked skeptically.

"There was this one time when these bar patrons got into a fistfight because they were fighting over whose turn it was to use the karaoke machine. Another time, we had to rescue a guy because the other customers were throwing beer bottles and shoes at him."

"Oh, come on, Dad," Robin said. "That's just two incidents with some drunk guys."

Dad looked at his son and the satyr. "I wasn't finished, son." He looked at me. "Shelly, what do you think of Strider's plan?"

"I say, Dad," I replied, "use your full power of veto. Eddie's against it too."

"That's the smartest thing he's done," Dad muttered under his breath.

Strider looked at Dad with big, brown Bambi eyes, but Dad shook his head. "No karaoke! End of discussion!" He pretended to brush away all of the karaoke dreams, past, present, and future. Then he headed back into the kitchen.

Eddie looked at Robin and Strider who were recovering from their shell shock. "Would you guys like something to drown your sorrows?" he asked them as an evil triumphant smirk crossed his lips.

Robin shrugged as he sat on the barstool next to me. "I'll have a bottle of cola," he said. Eddie quickly grabbed a soda from the under-the-counter, compact refrigerator and slid the glass bottle, Sam Malone-style across the counter to my brother.

After Robin opened the soda, he lifted the bottle to the vampire. "Been practicing, I take it?"

"Yep! I only knocked three glasses on the floor tonight so far."

Strider cleared off the counter and set the music machine on the floor next to his stool. "I'll have an eggplant mango shake with chocolate ice cream," he told the vampire.

I saw Eddie cringe. He hated making the satyr's special drink. He plopped two scoops of chocolate ice cream into the blender. Then he poured about one cup of milk into the blender, along with four mango slices. Finally, the shake was topped off with a purpley gloop which apparently was the eggplant syrup. He would have to hose the cup down and then bleach it out.

I watched as my boyfriend dumped the nuclear power plant mixture into a glass. "Oh!" A wave of nausea swept over me, but I held it back. "That looks nasty, Strider!"

"Don't knock it 'till you've tried it!" Strider replied as he took a long, luxurious sip of his drink.

"I prefer not seeing my lunch a second time, thank you," I said.

"Even though my sister completely dismissed your

karaoke machine idea," Robin said after he finished off his cola

and gestured for another glass, "she is right about your drink.

That just looks vile!"

"Yeah, tell me, Strider," I asked as I rested my left hand on

the side of my head, "how is that 'drink' in any way healthy?" My

friend is what I call "a neurotic health nut" who believes that

everything you eat must be all-natural, no matter how disgusting

it is. "Apparently, living past thirty is not high on your priority list."

Eddie rested his elbows on the countertop and set his

chin in the palms of his hands. He glanced at Strider's

concoction. "You know what your drink reminds me of?" The

question was directed to Strider, but the vampire was looking at

all of us. "The gutted innards of a dragon."

Strider looked at his glass full of purple chunks with

specks of orange floating around in a brownish sea. He pushed it

away from him. "Suddenly, I don't feel thirsty anymore. Do I still

have to pay for my special shake?"

"Look," Eddie told the satyr, "just because you came up with that liquid—I can't call it a proper 'shake'—doesn't mean that you get a specialized discount for it, Strider. It's still three-fifty." He rang up the gross milkshake on the register. Because Dad owns the restaurant, Robin and I don't have to pay for anything we get at the diner. The employees get a ten percent discount.

Strider reached into the back pocket of his blue jeans and pulled out his wallet. He handed the vampire a five-dollar bill. "I see you still haven't named my drink yet."

"I haven't thought of an appropriate one yet," my boyfriend answered as he dropped the change in the satyr's hand. He glanced over at me. *To tell the truth, I haven't given it much thought without gagging in the process*, he told me sublimely, He dumped the sludge down the garbage disposal, praying that it wouldn't get the appliance clogged up.

I decided to help him out. "I've got one, Eddie. The Self-Purging Milkshake?"

Strider glared at me as Eddie and Robin had a good laugh at my joke. "I'll keep that in mind, Shelly," Eddie said with a wink.

He was strongly considering my suggestion. "I was also thinking 'Toxic Waste Dump.'"

"Ooh, that's even better," I said. "Much more descriptive."

"Come on, Strider," Robin said as he gave his friend a pat on the back. "We should get going. It's almost time for the movie." As he and the goat man started to leave, he turned to me. "You want to come, Shelly?"

"No thanks," I said. "I'll just hang out here with Eddie."

"See you guys!" Robin waved good-bye to the vampire and me.

Strider just grumbled bye as he followed my brother out of the diner. Apparently, our innocent shake names were not quite what he was looking for.

"You're evil," I told Eddie once they had left.

"I'm evil?" he asked me. "Since when did you get a soul?"

"I bought it back from someone on eBay."

"Really now? What was the highest bid? One druci?"

"Very funny, Eddie." I grinned at him. Suddenly, my stomach growled, and I realized that I hadn't eaten supper yet.

Maybe, I would join Eddie on his lunch break. It wouldn't qualify as a date per se, but it would be a chance to eat something. "When are you going on lunch?"

Eddie checked his watch. "In about an hour or so. We can eat back in the kitchen or out here if you want. So, is this going to be our official first date?"

"If you want it to be, but having lunch while you are at work isn't really my idea of a romantic evening out."

Eddie nodded his head in agreement. He looked out from the corner of his eye and saw a couple of prospective customers. "What can I get for you folks?"

I sent Eddie a telepathic message letting him know I would talk with Dad. I went around the counter and grabbed the blender cup and Strider's glass to take back to the kitchen. The vampire shot me a grin of appreciation.

I dumped the dishes in the bubbly sink where Amelia was washing a few pots and pans. She looked down at the purple stains of the blender pitcher as it sank into the abyss of the foaming soap suds. "Don't tell me! Eddie made Strider's milkshake," she said as she lifted a soapy hand to push away a strand of her short black hair. She gave a short sigh. "I hope it comes out!" Doing the diner dishes was not exactly her favorite job at the diner. In fact, she loves to be the restaurant's hostess. I think because of her nurse's experience, she loves working with people. She always makes sure every customer at the diner is satisfied to the best of Anderson's Place's ability.

Wearing his white cook's uniform, Dad was flipping hamburgers layered with onions on the large, industrial oven. A memory floated in my mind of my father teaching his friend, Bruce, how to cook. Tears came to my eyes as feelings of missing my friends from Pembrook welled up in my heart. I wiped away the tears with the collar of my shirt. If Dad or Amelia asked why I was crying, I would tell them it was the onions. I walked up to the oven. "When are the burgers going to be ready?" I asked Dad as I inhaled the aroma of hamburger seasoned with barbeque sauce.

"In about fifteen minutes," Dad replied. He looked at me. "Why? Do you want one?"

"If it's okay, I'm eating lunch with Eddie." I reached for some lettuce that was on a huge plate near the oven.

"What are you doing?" Dad asked in mid-reach. "Don't touch the food!" One of his biggest pet peeves is people nibbling the food before he finishes cooking. He protects his food from fiendish hands like the guards patrolling the tomb of the unknown soldier.

"I'm just a little hungry," I explained. I held up my hands. "See, they're clean!" I decided to make myself useful. "Can I help with anything?"

"Oh, Shelly, could you cut up the bag of potatoes for us?" Amelia asked as she pulled the plug. The water gurgled loudly as it spun down the drain to its death. She wiped the excess water off her hands and smoothed down her black pants. She gave my dad a quick kiss on the lips before she left to go serve as hostess.

I pulled a bag of potatoes from of one of the wooden cabinets that Dad had installed himself when he was remodeling the diner. The wimpy paper bag broke, and potatoes scattered across the floor. So far, my night was going to Hell. Dad and I scrambled down to pick up all the runaway spuds. Finally, everything was all set to go. I grabbed a black-handled paring knife and matching peeler out of the utensil drawer. I worked here before I got a job as an assistant librarian at the Zephyr Public Library, and I know my way around pretty well.

Dad went back to flipping hamburgers. He looked frustrated and worried, but apparently, he didn't want to talk to me about it. A tired look was in his baby blue eyes. "Thanks for helping out, Shelly."

"No problem, Dad. I've got an hour to kill before Eddie goes on lunch." I looked around, noticing for the first time that the cook Dad had hired wasn't in the kitchen. "Where's the vampire cook—Frank, I think you said his name was—cook you hired?"

"I fired him last night. Eddie caught him stealing from one of the cash registers. At least, I can trust Eddie in that department." He gave a huge sigh. "This is the third cook I've had to fire in the last two weeks. What I would like to have is someone dependable, honest, and not a smart mouth."

"Eddie's dependable and honest, but he can be a smart

mouth sometimes."

Dad nodded. "I know, but I need Eddie out front where he

belongs. He's my best worker and a pretty good bouncer."

I nodded in agreement. I had seen my boyfriend throw out

some troublemakers in the diner a few times. He had done it

without any effort at all. Then I thought of the perfect cook to

work here. My heart sank as I realized how dumb an idea it was.

Bruce didn't even live in our reality, but I risked saying it aloud.

"What about Bruce?" My hand flew up to my mouth.

Dad paused in mid-flip. "You've been looking at your

picture album again, haven't you?"

I nodded but decided not to mention the dream. "I was just

thinking about how nice it would be to talk to Lisa again."

"Shelly, I miss being around all my friends back in

Pembrook, especially Bruce, but there's a very slim chance that

they'll ever come here." Even though he sounded confident in his

self-made decision, his voice seemed to have a tad bit of hope

that the wormhole would open up allowing his friends to come over. "Bruce would understand what's going on with—." His voice trailed off as soon as he met my eyes.

"I guess it was just wishful thinking," I replied as I set aside a skinless potato in the pile of three spuds that I had already peeled. "Dad," I said switching gears, "why don't you trust Eddie anymore?"

"He's supposed to be your guardian, but he nearly got you killed," Dad replied flatly without looking at me.

"What do you mean 'my guardian?' Dad, we're just dating, not pledging our lives to each other." Not that I would object to that. "I'm not a teenager, and Eddie's not my guardian, whatever that means. We're both adults, and I made the decision to raid the party. He was there when I really needed him."

"Guardians aren't supposed to fail."

I looked up at Dad. What on earth was he talking about? I had never heard him speak like this before. "Dad, Amelia approves of him."

"I don't think he's right for you."

My mouth dropped in surprise. "What!"

Dad said nothing.

"So, you don't want me seeing him?" I was totally confused. "You were fine with us being friends. So, what's the problem now?"

I must have been raising my voice because Dad glared at me. "Michelle, we're at the restaurant."

I placed my hands on my hips. "Dad, I am an adult, and I can see whoever I want. Right now that's Eddie. I don't know why you suddenly don't trust Eddie, but I trust him with my life. And you're just going to have to accept that." I waited for an answer but received nothing. Then I stalked out of the kitchen.

Eddie flagged me down from behind the counter. "How did it go?"

"Peachy!"

He grimaced. "That bad, huh?"

"He wasn't making any sense. He kept calling you my 'guardian.' He says 'guardians aren't supposed to fail.' Why is he suddenly all upset with us dating. I don't get it."

"Me neither." Eddie looked up to see Dad staring at us from the kitchen doorway. "Look, I need to get back to work. I'll call you later tonight to set up a date."

I managed a smile. "I'm looking forward to it." I gave the vampire a little wave which he returned and left the diner. As I climbed on Jordan, my thoughts turned from the argument with my dad back to the dream. I began wondering if I could help Lisa somehow. Which meant I would have to find a way to open a wormhole, with or without Eddie's help.

Chapter 3:

Eddie Falls Off My Ceiling

The next few days were uneventful. I found myself looking at the photo album about three times a day. I have no idea why I was looking it at so much. Maybe I was going through one of those phases in a person's life where they are stuck in the limbo of the past. I was even having that recurring dream.

The only other thing that happened to me was the growing amount of cobwebs in my house. The webs were silver and really thick, from a fly's point of view, I guess. The really weird thing was the only spider I saw was the same one that came from my yard-sale book. I had tried to kill it, but the book I threw at it must have missed it by a mile. I'm not a spider-hater, but things are never what they seem in a magical land, especially spiders. Good thing the book happened to be one of my own because the spine broke. I needed to go buy some new curtains, and I highly doubted that the discount linen store had those same navy blue curtains with the little white flowers for fifty percent off the original price. I'm cheap and proud of it.

On Tuesday night, I decided to clean up the spider's messes as I waited for Eddie to pick me up for our official first date. I had changed into a hot pink mock tee and black jeans. My vampire boyfriend and I were going out for pizza and an action/adventure movie that I had wanted to see for a long time. Critics gave it great reviews and so did Eddie who was just glad he didn't have to sit through a sappy romance.

I was standing on my dictionary, my thesaurus, and my chair to give myself an extra six inches when the vampire walked through the front door. "Hi, Eddie!" I said as I stood on my tiptoes and attempted to maintain my balance. I swatted at a silver thread with my purple feather duster.

Eddie looked up at me. He was wearing an untucked yellow polo shirt and blue Leviathan jeans along with a pair of white sneakers. Then his eyes followed down to the makeshift

death trap that I was standing on. "You know that's not really

safe, Shelly."

"Just be glad I'm not standing on a swivel chair," I replied.

Still on my tiptoes, I gave the annoying cobweb another vigorous

swat. That was not the wisest move on my part because I

suddenly lost my balance, mostly because of the lack of treads

on my Teva sandals. The vampire ran to my side like a knight in

shining armor rushing to the damsel in distress. He caught me in

his arms before the floor came up to hit me. "Are you wearing

cologne, Eddie?" I asked, sniffing the suddenly fragrant air.

"Yeah, I thought it would be nice for a change." He helped

me down off the chair. He was wearing expensive cologne called

Blue Ice, and it smelled good on him. He looked at the feather

duster in my hand. "Mind telling me what on earth you were

doing?"

"Cleaning out some cobwebs!"

"I think the cobwebs can wait 'till after our date."

"Just one more time, Eddie. Let me get at it once more."

The vampire threw up his hands in surrender. "All right, we can leave in another few minutes, but you aren't going back up there." He gestured for my feather duster which I gave him. Then he put it between his teeth, crouched down, and leaped up. He clung to the white, cathedral ceiling like a fly. Vampires can climb walls without outside help. Good thing the blood doesn't rush to his head, and he won't pass out. He took the duster out of his mouth and began to clean away the cobwebs. Oh, the things men will do for their girlfriends!

"While you're up there, Eddie, could you get the ones in the corner?" I asked, putting on my best Bambi eyes.

"Just be glad I like you, Shelly," he said with a slight grumble in his voice. When the feathers knocked away the nearest cobweb, something with eight, flailing legs leaped onto the handle of the duster. Eddie was about to shout in surprise when the creature that was about the size of a dollar bill (and that was just the body) cleared the handle and landed on his forehead. "Ohmigod!" he screamed as the feather duster plummeted to the floor so he could knock what I now realized was the troublesome spider off his face. Lifting his hands from the ceiling was his biggest mistake.

"Eddie, don't let go!" I shouted as I watched in horror as my boyfriend plunged to the floor.

THUD! "Ow!" Eddie said as he looked up at me from his position on the floor. The spider sped off his head and scurried to the safe haven of the sink.

"Are you all right?" I asked as I bent down to help him up. That was a stupid question to ask.

Eddie answered it for me. "No, Shelly, I just enjoy lying on your kitchen floor with my back in throbbing pain." He took my hand and pulled himself to his feet. He placed his hands on his hips and gently leaned back. "God, that hurt!" he said through clenched teeth (clenched fangs?) as he winced in pain.

"How long will it take for you to heal?" I asked. Vampires are fast healers, but even I was unsure how long it would take a bruised back to heal. I felt really bad for what happened to my boyfriend. If I hadn't asked him to clean off those stupid strings, Eddie wouldn't be hunched over like Quasimodo.

"With good luck, I'll be fine in a half-hour or so."

"I'm so sorry about your injured back, Eddie! I shouldn't have asked you—."

"It's not your fault, Shelly, entirely!" he replied with a wicked grin. I felt better knowing the fact that Eddie wasn't ticked off at me and still wanted to go out. He hobbled over to the bathroom to look for something to help the healing along. "Shelly, where do you keep your Advil?"

"I don't have any, but there's some aspirin in the medicine cabinet!" I said as I grabbed a glass from my china cabinet. I poured him a glass of water. Like most normal people on the face of the planet, Eddie likes to take his pills with water or other liquids.

He came back with three aspirin in his cupped hand. Gratefully, he washed down the medicine with the water.

"Do you want to sit down?" I asked.

"Actually, more like lie down," Eddie said as he wandered into my living room. I followed him to the couch where he promptly laid down on his back and shut his eyes. "Mind if I take up residence on your couch for a little bit?" he asked me as an afterthought.

I hesitated. "Uh, sure. No problem!" I jammed my hands into the pockets of my jeans and stood around for a few minutes looking stupid. Then I had a grandiose idea. I grabbed my laptop and turned it on as I sat down on the floor up against the couch. One of my two purple pillows was cushioning Eddie's head. "Can I have the pillow that's keeping your butt elevated?" I asked him.

Eddie groaned in melodramatic pain as he lifted himself up and tossed the pillow at me. He rolled over onto his side and propped himself on his elbow. He looked over my shoulder as I clicked on the link to the Internet. "Mind telling me what you are doing?"

"I've decided to try to identify that spider," I said as I sat on the already warm pillow. I went on my favorite search engine, FindIt.com, and typed in the word "spider." Within seconds, sixty million links to sixty million sites popped up on my computer screen. This would take a while. I really needed to narrow down my search. Like, find only one million sites.

"Why are you researching this spider? It's like you have got a grudge against it or something."

"Something's not right with it. You got a good look at that spider, Eddie. Did you see how big it was? Because the last time I saw the thing, it was the size of the cap on a milk bottle. So, what did it look like?"

"Nice, adding insult to injury! The only thing I remember was that the spider had eight legs."

"Ooh," I said with mock sincerity, "that really narrows it down quite a bit."

"Well, excuse me! I wasn't really looking for identifying marks when it leaped on my face."

I rolled my eyes and chose to ignore him. "I'm pretty sure it's gotten bigger."

"Bigger?" He raised a skeptical eyebrow.

"Yeah, I think it's growing." I glanced at Eddie who gave one of his famous What-are-you-on looks. "Does that sound crazy?"

"Yes! Spiders don't grow in just a few days."

"Then how do they go from baby to adult?"

"Let me rephrase that last statement: Adult spiders don't grow bigger in just a few days."

I sulked at my boyfriend's smart-alec remark. I think his pessimistic statement was a result of the pain he was in (which was not only going to be centered on his back if he continued riding the train of cynicism). "Or maybe it's just my imagination," I remembered the rainbow colors on the spider. "Did it have lots of colors on it?"

Eddie shrugged. "Yeah, I think so." Then he gave an evil chuckle. "Heh, heh. You have a psychotic spider living with you. Bet it's the first time you've ever seen a rainbow-colored spider."

"You're right—." Then I realized what Eddie had just said. I looked at him. "You mean a crazy or colorful spider?"

"Colorful. Why? What did I say?"

"You mean psychedelic," I replied as I playfully punched the vampire in the arm. My laptop nearly slid off my stretched out legs when I turned to hit Eddie. I reached out to grab it by the cover. My laptop landed on the carpet with a soft thump. I gave a short intake of breath as I feared my five hundred dollar computer had broken. My fanged boyfriend's fit of laughter wasn't helping the situation.

"Serves you right for making fun of the injured," Eddie replied as he wiped away the tears that were streaming down his cheeks. After being a vampire for who knows how long, he's easily amused. His back was almost healed. Laughter is the best medicine, apparently. Even when it's at someone else's expense.

I set my laptop back in its previous position. "Since your back's almost healed, we can head out on our date," I told him. It's hard for me to stay mad at Eddie especially since I turn to putty whenever he looks into my eyes.

Eddie sat up. "Give me a few more minutes. I promise, no more smart remarks while you're searching the Web." Another wisecrack almost passed through his lips, but he didn't say it. He patted the cushion next to him. "Come sit with me, Shelly."

I joined him on the couch and set my very warm laptop on my lap (what a concept!). I felt Eddie's arm slip around me as I subconsciously cuddled up to him. A few weeks ago, this would have been awkward, but not now. I smiled at my boyfriend as I typed in the keywords rainbow-colored spider, setting quotation marks around the phrase and hit enter. "Yes!" I gave Eddie a high five as I got three million hits this time. I was so proud of myself, as was the vampire. Actually, he really wanted to get going on our date.

Among the million sites, we found useless junk about spider monkeys, spider veins, and spider plants (which I would probably kill within the first week if I ever owned one). Finally, Eddie suggested that I click onto a website called spiderzrkool.com. Even though the site had been up for about six months, it was certainly still under construction. The homepage had red lettering on a pink background which Eddie and I could barely read. The links were even more useless. Half of them were broken or rerouted the user back to the main page. Maybe searching the Internet for spiders wasn't the best idea at the moment. I shut down the computer and hopped off the couch. "I think your back's fine, Eddie." I grabbed one of his hands and helped him off the couch. "Let's head out!"

"Fine by me," Eddie said.

I grabbed my purse off the kitchen table, and we walked outside where Eddie's bright green motorcycle was waiting patiently for us. This one was a little bit smaller than his last motorcycle which was now resting in pieces somewhere in the heart of the town dump. Don't get me wrong! My boyfriend's an extremely safe motorcyclist. His last bike was actually blasted apart by an angry sorcerer who also happened to be a mafia kingpin here in Zephyr. I climbed back and put on the black helmet. Eddie tightened the strap on his helmet and started up the bike. I put my arms around his waist as we sped down the road to Parrilla's Pizza, the newest pizza parlor in town.

The night was the best that I've had in a long time. Eddie and I shared laughs and a good time over extra cheese pizza and soda.

"So," I said as I was recovering from a funny story that Eddie told me, "how long have you been a vampire?"

Eddie hesitated for a minute. "Well, I was twenty-five when I was turned almost forty years ago."

"Then that would make you—." I paused as I did the math in my head. "Sixty-five! You're old enough to be my grandfather!"

"See? That's why I don't normally tell my dates how old I actually am. It kind of ruins the moment."

"Well, I think older men are more mature and much more handsome."

He smiled at me as he drank his soda.

"So, how did you become a vampire?"

The smile faded as his eyes got misty. "It's a long story."

"We've got time."

"I don't want to talk about it," he said.

"Sorry, I didn't realize it would upset you."

"It's alright. It's just a very painful topic." He decided to change the subject. "So, have you had any more dreams?"

"Just the same one. I really think Lisa's in danger."

"Can you prove it?"

"No, but I can feel it."

Eddie gave me a skeptical look. "Are we talking 'women's intuition' here?"

"I guess so." I paused and took a deep breath. "I'm going to try to open another wormhole."

Eddie took a bite out of his pizza before answering. "Ambitious. Want some help pulling it off?"

I nodded. "I got the cards, and I found a spell online that I can use." I noticed the dubious look in the vampire's eyes. "The website's legit. Plus, at least, I can try." I added with a shrug.

"Let me know when and where, and I'll be there."

See, Dad, I said to myself, *you're wrong about Eddie.* The rest of our dinner went perfectly, as did the movie. I don't remember what the plot was though. There was a lot of action and explosions, but maybe that was my heart pounding as Eddie held my hand throughout the entire movie.

By the time he dropped me off at my house, it was almost eleven. We sat on the bike. The moon was hanging up in the clear sky with millions of twinkling stars. I tried to find some of the various constellations. "What's that one?" I asked Eddie as I pointed to a cluster of stars that looked like a stick drawing of a cat with serious disfigurements.

"That's the Tiger," Eddie told me. "The story goes that the elf king who founded Zephyr fought some vicious giants like a tiger. When he died, the ancient Welkies sent his body to the stars in the form of a tiger."

I looked back up at the cluster. "I think the Welkie must not have been very artistic. Because it looks like a four-year-old rearranged it." I paused. "I think the stars are gorgeous tonight. They're so bright." I leaned against the vampire's shoulder.

He looked at me with surprise. "I didn't know you liked looking at the stars. Have you ever been to the planetarium here?"

"The last time I went to one, my ninth-grade class got kicked out."

"Wow! You bad girl! What did you do?"

"I was innocent, but my fellow classmates were throwing spitballs and both empty and half-full soda cans and being rambunctious in general."

"Was Robin involved in the revelries?"

I shook my head. "No, he was out sick but pretty upset that he missed all the fun." Robin and I had been in the same grades all through school. "Now that I think about it that was the last field trip I ever went on."

Eddie smiled at me. "Well, maybe we should make the planetarium one of our dates. Just no spitballs!"

"That would be so cool, Eddie! How about doing that for our next date?"

He smacked his forehead with the palm of his hand. "Oh, shoot!" he exclaimed. "I just remembered something. Do you have plans tomorrow night?"

"No, I just have to work 'till seven, after that I'm free. Why?"

"My aunt and uncle invited us over for dinner."

"That would be great!" I really like the Count and Countess Von Stoker. They are a very nice and very wealthy couple of vampires. They live in a huge mansion on the outskirts of Zephyr. Even though the Count and Countess come from a royal bloodline of vampires, they have as much power and influence as the King of Rock and Roll. "What should I wear?"

"Something like what you're wearing right now would be great. I can pick you up from work if you want."

"Sure!" We sat in a peaceful silence watching the stars when one went shooting overhead. I closed my eyes. "Make a wish!" I murmured.

Eddie shot me a puzzled look. "Are you serious?"

I shrugged. "I'm just being silly."

"Let me try." Eddie closed his eyes for a long moment. "There. I made my wish."

"What did you wish for?" I asked leaning forward with my hands clasped together. I didn't want to read his mind. Instead, I wanted to hear him tell me his wish.

He leaned toward me and put his hand on my neck. I was surprised as he pulled me close to him. I didn't want to resist. His fangs retracted as he kissed me on the lips. It wasn't a quick kiss, nor was it a long, passionate one. It was just right. My first kiss had been the perfect kiss. Eddie pulled back from me as his fangs appeared back over a big grin. "Got what I wished for."

I think my heart skipped a couple of beats. The heat rushed to my face. It was a good kind of embarrassment. Like the kind you get when you walk into a surprise birthday party or when you get your dream job, but so much better.

"What did you wish for?" Eddie asked bringing me out of my trance.

Even though vampires can't really hypnotize people, I sure felt like it at the present moment. "It's dumb," I said. Well, compared to Eddie's wish, it was the whole truth and nothing but the truth.

"Come on, tell me."

"Well," I hesitated for a moment, "I wished to see my friend, Lisa, again."

"Maybe it'll come true. My wish did." He was so proud of himself for his cleverness.

"Yeah, you kind of forced your wish to come true."

"I don't remember any kind of ground rules for making wishes."

"It was a great wish," I said beaming with joy. We hopped off the motorcycle and walked to my front door. "Maybe you're right." The blank look on Eddie's face told me that he had no idea what I was talking about. "About my wish," I answered as I unlocked the door. "Heck, this is a land of magic. Maybe it will come true."

"It just might," the vampire said as he kicked a clump of grass with his toe. He leaned in, but quickly pulled back. He didn't want to go too fast. We told each other that we would take things slowly. "Well, I should let you go get some sleep. I'll see you at the library tomorrow." He waved good-bye and walked back to his motorcycle.

I watched him drive away and closed the door behind me. "He kissed me!" I squealed in girlish delight. I felt like the kid who got the most Halloween candy. Suddenly, I began twirling around in my kitchen as I belted out the lyrics of the song "I Could Have Danced All Night" from the musical *My Fair Lady*. This was one of those times I wished I could tell Lisa all the juicy details. I put on my pajamas and collapsed into bed. My mind was racing with everything that had transpired in the last half hour.

Chapter 4:

It Can't Be Killed, Captain!

The next day I walked to work wearing a light purple knit tee and a pair of beige jeans. Since Eddie was picking me up from work, I decided not to go for the red carpet look. I told no one about my night until lunch. I was eating some noodles in a cup. *Time for me to go grocery shopping*, I told myself as I realized how nasty and utterly tasteless the flimsy pasta was. I had told Cricket earlier that week that I was going on my first date with Eddie.

"So, how did it go?" she asked me from across the oval table in the staff room.

"Good!" I said with a big grin. "We went to dinner and a movie. It was fun." I told all about my night, leaving out the part about Eddie's wish.

Cricket listened intently, but she was waiting to ask me something. "Did he kiss you?" she finally blurted out. My friend gets down to the brass tacks really fast.

"I'll never tell." Probably the big, sappy smile on my face gave away my secret.

"He did, didn't he?"

"Yeah, I guess so." I shrugged as if it were no big deal. The noodles were slipping off my fork, and I tried to eat them before they landed in a Styrofoam cup with a big splash. "Oh, crap!" A dark stain about the size of a quarter appeared on the front of my shirt. I took a brown industrial napkin and ended up grinding the stain in more deeply. Man, this was my favorite shirt! Hopefully, Eddie wouldn't mind swinging by my house so I could change into something that didn't scream hopeless slob. Cricket was about to ask me more date details when the phone in the staff room rang. Someone answered it and told the fairy it was for her. I smiled to myself as I carefully ate the rest of my soup. At least Cricket wasn't interrogating me anymore about my date.

It was six o'clock in the evening, and I was working at the check-out desk at the library. Everything was going smoothly until I saw Mr. Folletto walk up in a huff. He was one of my least favorite patrons. He hadn't been in for a few months, and now I had to deal with him. Lucky me. The old elf leaned his wrinkled, angry face into my personal bubble. "I want to know why I can't get on the computers here!" he demanded.

"Let's see what going on. May I see your library card?" I asked calmly.

"I don't have it with me!"

"Well, could I see some kind of identification?" Even though I knew who he was, I'm a stickler for library policy. He reluctantly gave me his Zephyr I.D. card, and I pulled up his record. I noticed that he had about thirty dollars in fines. "Mr. Folletto, the reason why you were denied access to the computers is that you have $30.85 in fines."

"How is that possible! I haven't been here since March! I brought back all my books!" He slammed his fist down on the desk. Everyone on the first floor must have heard him because they stopped what they were doing and stared at me and the "happy" patron.

"Sir, I know that, but you brought the books back late. So, your fines just added up. In order to be allowed on computers, all fines have to be under five druci."

"Don't interrupt me!" he growled.

I looked up from Mr. Folletto to see Eddie standing a few feet behind the elf. *Hi!* I told the vampire mentally. If I spoke aloud to anyone else, Mr. Folletto most likely would go completely postal.

Need some help with this guy? Eddie telecommunicated back to me. He smoothed out his black and red polo in order to try to impress me. Unfortunately, I was too busy dealing with Satan to appreciate the gesture.

I shook my head. *Hang around here just in case.* I watched the vampire pick up a book and pretend to read it. A technique he must have learned as a spy. "Look at me when I'm talking to you!" snapped the elf angrily as my head stealthily turned back to face him. His voice raised a couple more octaves. "I brought those books back! I want to get on the computers to check my email."

"I know, sir, but you brought the books back late. In order to get on the computers, your fines have to be under fifteen druci," I told him, my patience wearing thin. What was I not explaining to him? You brought books back late, your fines accumulated, and you couldn't go on the computers until the fees are under fifteen druci. What was so hard to understand?

"I brought back those books so I don't need to pay any kind of stupid fine!"

I crossed my arms and said in a calm, steady voice, "Mr. Folletto, you need to calm down and lower your voice right now. I can't help you if—."

"NO!" Mr. Follotto reached over to grab me, but I instinctively took two steps backward. "You listen to me!" he screamed. He's gone mad, stark raving mad! The last thing I wanted was some psychopath sending me to the morgue on a gurney.

"Buddy, you need to back off."

Mr. Folletto whirled around to face the vampire. "This is none of your business!" he snarled at Eddie. He raised his cane above his head. I thought he might actually beat the vampire into a jelly.

Eddie swiftly reached out and grabbed the cane in mid-swing. "Put it down," he ordered calmly as he lowered the cane with all his strength. Even though he had let it go, he was watching Mr. Folletto and his walking stick like a hawk. "Now just because you didn't pay your fines, you don't have to get angry at her. It's your problem, not hers."

"If you keep this up, Mr. Folletto, I will ask you to leave the building," I told the elf firmly. I felt more confident with Eddie standing nearby. Plus, I had enough of the guy's crap already.

Mr. Folletto grabbed his ID card from the desk and stalked out the door without another word. There's the door! Don't let it hit you in the keister on the way out!

Eddie walked up to the desk with a smirk. "It's not every day that I get a chance to meet the library patron from Hell."

"But which layer?" I challenged.

"Oh, the seventh layer, definitely! But you handled him quite well." He reached into the back pocket of his blue jeans for his wallet. "While I'm here, can you check to see if I have fees on my library card?"

I pulled up Eddie's record. "You got five druci in fines," I told him. I looked at the details of the fines. They were for books that my boyfriend brought back three years ago, but he never paid the fines. "These fines are really old, Eddie! When was the last time you checked out a book?" Here he was dating a librarian, and he rarely darkened the doors of a library. I shook my head sadly as Eddie shrugged helplessly. I would help him out this one time, but he was going to pay. "Because your fines are so old, I'll waive them, but you're going to have to do something for me," I told him as I kept my word.

Eddie grimaced. "I don't think I'm going to like this, Shelly."

"Oh, well!" I said with a shrug. "Can you get me as many books on spiders as you can?" Eddie had no idea how to find books categorized in the Carnahan Decimal System, a Zephyrian classification similar to the Dewey Decimal System. I gave him the best suggestion possible. "Ask one of the reference librarians to help you. They're really nice and helpful." I shot him a sappy smile as I held back a snicker.

Eddie shook his head at me. I was so kind to load him with my spider problems. Come to think of it, he was involved. If there were a purple heart for injuring your back while ridding the world of troublesome cobwebs, he would have earned a boxful of them. It didn't take long for the vampire to come back with his arms full of books. He set them on the desk in front of me. "Happy?" he asked.

"You're the best, Eddie," I said as I pulled up my own record. "I'll put them on my card." I started to check the books with the scanner which was actually working this time. I was so glad that I didn't need to hand key in any of the book barcodes. That just takes forever. "Due back in three weeks!"

"Yeah, but you're bringing them back!" he told me.

"Don't worry. Oh, by the way, can we swing by my house before we go to your aunt and uncle's?"

"Why?"

I pointed to the stain on my shirt. "I spilled some food on my shirt today. I keep looking down, thinking that it's getting bigger."

Eddie raised his eyebrows. "If the stain was really growing, I'd be more concerned about the food you were eating."

"Noodles in a cup," I explained.

"That would be cause for concern. I'll be waiting for you in my cuke car." He waved bye and walked out the front door. Being a great mechanic, Eddie has built eight cars, all in different shapes of fruits and vegetables. My personal favorite is the "picklemobile," a dark green, four-door car that looks like a beat-up pickle. Eddie insists that it looks like a cucumber, but I think he just picked the wrong color paint when he was building it.

A little after seven, I spotted the ugly car. Looking both ways before crossing the street as my mother had always told me, I darted across Main Street to the parking lot where Eddie was waiting for me. I opened the back door of the car and heaved my green and white canvas bag behind my seat. I looked over at the vampire who was reading one of the books I had checked out. "Find anything interesting?" I asked him as I slid into the front passenger seat and buckled up.

Eddie put down the book. "I think I have looked for your elusive spider in almost every one of these ten books you had me get—."

"And?" I asked him as we pulled out of the parking lot.

"I found absolutely nothing remotely similar to the spider."

I groaned aloud as I leaned against the headrest. "Maybe I just have spider problems."

"Ya think?"

I nodded. It's only a short drive to my house. Once the car came to a stop in my little sixteen-foot-long driveway, I gathered up my canvas bag and the library books and went into my house. Eddie said he'd wait out in the car for me, just as long as I was quick about changing my shirt. I set my pile of stuff on the kitchen table and went into my bedroom to change. Glancing at the living room, I noticed silver balls the size of baby carrots hanging from the ceiling. *That was strange!* I said to myself. *They weren't there when I left this morning.* This was craptastic! The spider either invited its buddies over or those silver balls were holding eight-legged, spider babies. Either way, this was not a good sign. I gave a little shiver as I changed my shirt and hurried out of the house.

Once I was back in the car, Eddie backed out the driveway. "That shirt looks great on you, Shelly!" he said admiring my deep purple, sleeveless sweater.

I blushed a bit. "Thanks. Twenty bucks at Merlot's!"

"Not a bad bargain!"

"So, when are your aunt and uncle expecting us?"

Eddie checked his watch. "In about an hour or so."

"Good. Can we stop someplace to get a bug bomb?"

"A bug bomb?"

I nodded. "I discovered a bunch of silver, thread-like sacks hanging from my ceiling. I figure that I have to get rid of them before they hatch and infest my apartment. The place needs good fumigation."

"And you said it with an evil chuckle in your voice." He pressed down on the gas pedal, gently, so he wouldn't exert the engine too much as he started to pull out of my driveway. Once the car goes past sixty-five it starts to shake violently as if it were in the middle of a California earthquake.

"I did not. I'm just not fond of the idea of waking up one morning with spiders crawling all over my face."

"You're a sadistic spider killer."

"Spider killer, yes. Sadistic, no."

We heard a soft thump. I peered over the hood of the car. "Did you hit something, Eddie?" I asked looking around for a body, providing it wasn't plastered to the grill of the car.

"I don't think so. It's probably just the muffler. I was having some trouble with it earlier today." His statement didn't surprise me one bit. The old picklemobile was falling apart at the seams. I think the vampire has replaced the muffler about five times. He refuses to give up the flying dumpster for sentimental reasons.

A little later we walked into Garden of Eden Grocery, and I made a beeline for the home and garden center as Eddie trailed behind me. I located the bug sprays and began looking at the back of the cans. "Not that one. Too short. Nah."

Eddie leaned against a pillar with his arms crossed watching me nearly destroying the shelf. "Looking for a particular bug bomb?"

"One that kills spiders instantly!" I picked up a can and read the back. "Ooh, this is what I need." I tossed the can to the vampire.

He looked the can over. "'Kills all insects and spiders in 24 hours. Highly toxic to humans and pets.' I hope you're not going to stay at your house when you set this off."

"Of course not, Eddie. I mean, I wouldn't mind watching the spider die, but I have my health to consider. I was planning on setting it off before I leave for work tomorrow and then camping out at Dad's until the fumes have cleared."

Eddie nodded sagely. "Wise counsel."

"You bet your bottom dollar, it is!"

"Who are you, Little Orphan Annie?"

One would think a house owned by two vampires would be like something off the set of *The Munsters.* But that wasn't the case with Count Konrad Von Stoker, and his wife, Phoebe. The estate is set back a good 200 yards away from the main road with a long, winding driveway. The old four-story Victorian has been in the Von Stoker family for hundreds of generations and still has not lost its glamour with its dark gray siding and blue shutters around each of its sixty windows. After parking the car, we walked up to the front door.

Countess Phoebe Von Stoker opened up the huge oak doors for us. "Eddie," the vampire said as she put an arm around her nephew. She reminds me of Morticia Adams with her long black hair and her yellow and black sundress. "It's so good having you and Shelly over for dinner. Please, come in."

Just then she stopped rather abruptly and watched something dart across the doorstep, but she shrugged it off. She ushered us into the dark hallway with scarlet walls and into the large dining room where the table was set with black and orange dishes. Two pitchers were filled to the brim with peach tea and ice cubes. "Sit down, both of you," the Countess told us as she pointed near the end of the table. "I need to help Ramon in the kitchen." She hurried off to help their chef, the werecat Ramon Mashwarohn, with the rest of supper. Ramon is the Emeril Lagasse of the undead, and the Von Stokers were fortunate enough to have him in their employment.

I eased into the hunter green, lightly padded chair that Eddie had pulled out for me. My nose caught the scent of vegetable stir-fry seasoned with soy sauce that drifted in from the kitchen. I hoped Eddie couldn't hear my stomach rumbling with hunger. Not surprisingly as those disgusting noodles I had for lunch weren't all that filling.

The doors to the dining room opened, and a balding, plump vampire entered the dining area. He smiled, showing his capped fangs, at Eddie and me. "How are you doing?" Count Konrad Von Stoker said as he gave the other vampire a great bear hug. He reached over and shook my hand with his beefy hand. Unlike his wife, Count was not born a vampire. In his first life, the Count had been a very overweight ruler in the olden days of Zephyr. Over three hundred and fifty years ago he had been run over by a produce cart after being bitten by a vampire cow (I kid you not, they do exist.) Now, he is doomed to wander the fields and gardens of unsuspecting fruits and vegetables in the dead of the night. His wife calls it a blessing than a curse. "How is Eddie's favorite librarian?" the Count asked me.

I tried hard not to blush. I glanced over at Eddie who was struggling not to smirk at me. He had told his uncle that pick-up line. "I'm doing well," I answered. "How's your investment firm doing?"

The Count smiled as he sat down across from us. "It's going very well. I just hired a new partner." Even though he is very wealthy with the inheritance that his great-great-grandfather left him, the older vampire used some of the money to start an investment firm helping out brand-new businesses. In fact, my dad was one of his first clients.

"Who did you hire?" Eddie asked his uncle.

"Your cousin, Luken. He just graduated from Shadowlands University last month. He's moving here in a few weeks. Do you think you and Dirk can let him stay with you until he finds a place to live?"

"I don't know. I'll have to talk to Dirk about it," Eddie replied reluctantly. I jumped into his mind to find out why he was so hesitant about having his cousin stay with him. Apparently, Luken was known to his cousins as a bit of a player, and I'm not talking about sports.

Soon the Countess came out with a huge platter loaded with steaming strawberry biscuits. She was followed by Ramon carrying a huge bowl of vegetable stir-fry I had smelled earlier. "The jalapeño potatoes are going to be ready in just a few minutes, Konrad," the big, burly orange werecat told our host in a thick accent that sounded as if he had come from the Cajun district of New Orleans. As soon as he set the dish on the table, he hurried back to the kitchen to tend to his creation.

The Countess sat down next to her husband as she passed us the biscuits. I wanted to eat every one of those strawberry goodnesses, but I politely took just one. The last thing I needed was to act like the lions on the Serengeti. I took my butter knife and helped myself to the honey butter. The first luscious bite sent me to a higher dimension of Biscuit World. I sent Eddie a mental message asking if his aunt would be willing to give Dad the recipe.

You can ask her, but I know for a fact that Aunt Phoebe would never give out her secret family recipes, Eddie replied.

It couldn't hurt to try. "Countess?" I asked, unsure of what to call her? Mrs. Von Stoker. That didn't sound right. Especially addressing a member of royalty. Aunt Phoebe? It's a little bit too early in my relationship with Eddie and a little too weird. "These biscuits are so good! My dad would love to have the recipe for his restaurant."

The Countess smiled politely showing her capped fangs. "Unfortunately, Shelly, I didn't make them. Ramon did."

"Oh?" Eddie and I said at the same time. I didn't press the issue. As my dad always says, "A great chef never shares his secrets." I think you can say the same for any occupation. Anyway, I didn't want to get on Ramon's bad side. He could be a bouncer in any club in Zephyr.

Eddie scooped out a couple of spoonfuls of the stir-fry on my plate before serving himself. "I got to meet one of Shelly's favorite patrons," he told his aunt and uncle.

"Actually, the guy's more like the library patron from Hell," I explained. I told them what had happened. "The guy's a ticking time bomb. One word can set him off."

The Count shook his head. "Perhaps the library should invest in some bouncers," he suggested. "I'm sure Eddie wouldn't mind doing it."

Oh, yeah! I could definitely see my boyfriend kicking some annoying-patron-butt. "Nah, we rarely have trouble there," I said as I took a sip of my peach tea. "Anyway, our budget couldn't afford it."

"Or perhaps Ramon would do it for the library on his nights off," the Countess said.

"Yeah, Ramon's not scared of anything," Eddie replied. He has known the werecat for quite some time. The chef used to be a professional fighter before he turned in his boxing gloves for a chef's hat.

Just then we heard a loud crash and the werecat cursing in the kitchen. "Out! Out! Démon à huit pattes!" He ran into the dining room where we all stopped what we were doing to gawk at his apron sprinkled with flecks of potatoes and pieces of red hot peppers. "Konrad, Phoebe!" he bellowed. "You have a gigantic spider in your kitchen! It leaped down from the shelves and knocked over my pot, filled to the brim with my creation. Now, it's utterly ruined!"

The Countess was in shock. A huge, unwanted insect was destroying the kitchen she designed herself. She looked over at me as if she, too, could read my mind. Or was it because sweat beads were suddenly streaming down my face like I had just done a twenty-minute workout?

"Uh, Ramon?" I asked hesitantly, "what did this spider look like?"

"Let me show you," Ramon said as he held out his furry palm. Slowly, a hologram of a spider about the size of a small rat appeared. His magical ability showed us every little detail, including the colored stripes on its back in the same order.

Eddie and I exchanged nervous, knowing glances. Oh, crap! The spider followed us here. Its leaping on the car was most likely the thump we heard on the drive. "So, what happened to it?" I asked.

"I cut it in half with a huge butcher knife, but then it grew back together again!"

I looked over at the Countess as she thought in horror about the huge knife indentation in the newly cleaned stove. I was puzzled at the failed assassination attempt. What kind of spider grows back together after it is cut in half? With a butcher knife, no less! "Where is it now?" I asked the chef.

Ramon didn't have to answer because everyone was looking at the ceiling. I followed their gaze as the spider crawled across the plaster. Then it did a long jump onto the pitcher of iced tea. A sea of brown liquid splashed all over the pure white tablecloth. But Anansi wasn't done yet. He or she (I can't tell the gender of spiders) scurried across the table, knocking everything in its path. Glasses shattered and food flew across the table as we tried to chase after the destroyer of dinner. The Count took his dinner fork and stabbed it, but the thing ran with the utensil stuck deep in its back, green goo dripping behind it. I even tried to hit it with my purse, but the only result I got was spilling all the contents on the floor and table.

Eddie threw out both of his palms facing the indestructible spider. "Nebulae!" he snarled. Two huge balls of white fire shot out from his hands and hit their target. I thought for sure that would finish the spider off, but no! It scurried away as if nothing could hurt it. It leaped off the edge of the table taking the now flaming tablecloth with it. The Countess ran into the kitchen to get the fire extinguisher. Finally, it did a four-foot jump onto a window ledge. Eddie threw another one of his nebula spells which actually blew out the window and allowed the spider to escape.

It was fairly silent for the next hour as I helped the Countess clean up the mess. Eddie and his uncle had gone to get some plywood for a temporary replacement window. I thought it wise not to mention to my boyfriend's aunt that I had a pretty good feeling of where the spider-thing came from. Not exactly the best thing to bring up if you're counting on your significant other's family to accept you.

As we drove back to my house, Eddie and I were thinking about the catastrophe in complete silence. It was way too quiet for me. Finally, I had to break the ice. "Nice job on setting the tablecloth ablaze. You know your aunt bought it on sale just for this occasion."

"Dang it! My fire spells are pretty deadly, but that thing didn't even get singed."

"I just don't get it," I said, resting my head on the headrest. "What kind of spider can survive getting cut in half, a fork stabbing, and four fireballs being thrown at it? I know that Zephyr isn't exactly the most normal land, but spiders aren't supposed to do that!" I paused and looked at Eddie. He has taught me so much about the magical oddities in this city, and I'm still learning. "Are they?"

"I have never seen any kind of insect doing any kind of the stuff we saw tonight." Eddie pulled into my driveway. We sat in the car for a few quiet moments. "Sorry about our date not going so well," the vampire told me as we got out of the car. He walked me to my front door holding my hand. "I'll make it up to you, I promise."

I unlocked and opened my front door and was about to step inside when Eddie gently grabbed my elbow. Slowly, he pulled me closer to him. I nearly melted into his arms as he gently kissed me on the lips for the second time in two nights, fangs and all. I had to return the kiss. A minute or so later I reluctantly pulled away from him. "Ah, have a good night!" I managed to utter the dumb phrase.

Eddie smiled at me. "You too. Sleep well."

Oh, I will, I told myself, *I'll be having sweet dreams with you in them*. He waved good-bye as he headed off to his car. Even though the night had been pretty rotten, the last few minutes were the best that a girl could ask for. I closed the door and slid down to the floor. "He kissed me again!" I said as I clapped my hands happily. I finally went to bed. I fell asleep thinking about the second and first kiss.

Chapter Five:

My Wish is Granted, Sort of.

The following night I collected the cards and the spell I had printed off the web and met Eddie behind the diner. The weatherman had predicted correctly for a downpour. Unfortunately, I hadn't, and my blue shirt and jeans were drenched.

"Ready?" Eddie asked me as soon as he moved his motorcycle well out of the way. He shrugged off his green windbreaker which he was wearing over his royal blue shirt and black jeans. "Do you want to borrow my coat?"

I nodded. "Maybe we should move toward the end of the parking lot."

"You worried?"

"No," I lied. I was going to attempt to open a magical wormhole for the first time in my life. I zipped up Eddie's jacket and dug my hands into the pockets. "I just think we should play it safe."

Eddie nodded. "Good idea!" We walked to the edge of the concrete and both knelt on the grass. "So, any sign of the spider?"

I shook my head. "Haven't seen it at all. I'm hoping it ran away in fear of us." From the look on Eddie's face, I knew he wasn't buying my explanation. "Or maybe, it gave up on me and went to annoy someone else. I have high hopes. Please don't dash them."

"The bomb should kill it if it tries to get back into your apartment. The back of the container declared it was highly toxic."

The back door opened, and Dad stepped outside. "What's going on? Eddie, get back inside. Your break's over."

The vampire looked up at my dad. "Give me another few minutes. I'm helping Shelly out."

Dad narrowed his eyes at Eddie. "What are you trying to do?"

"Dad, I'm going to try to open a wormhole."

"Why?"

I hesitantly told my father about the dream. He didn't seem surprised about it, but since he used to be a cop, he had a great poker face. "I really think they're in danger."

"Just be careful!" Dad said.

Eddie and I looked at each other with surprise. Dad had more confidence in my serious lack of wormhole opening experience than I did. "Okay, here it goes," I recalled the lines from the spell and closed my eyes. "'Carry on, my wayward soul. There'll be peace when you are whole. Open up the window of possibility. Allow your mind to set you free.'" Okay, that made sense. The last phrase made no sense at all, but I said it aloud anyway. "'How does it feel to be without a home? Like a complete unknown? Like a rolling stone?'" Who wrote this? Some idiot who spliced together a couple of rock songs and called it a spell?

The wind around me began to whip around stronger as a purple light began to glow brightly behind me. Glancing over my shoulder, the wormhole that I saw five years ago was spinning around at an incredibly high speed. The lid on one of the blue dumpsters behind the diner flew open. Two garbage bags were lifted out by invisible hands and hurled towards Eddie and me.

"Shelly!" Dad cried. Stretching out his arm across the parking lot, he pulled us out of the way of the flying garbage bags before they disappeared into the wormhole. Seconds later, a middle-aged man and a man and a woman in their twenties tumbled from the portal. Dad ran over to check on the newcomers right after the wormhole closed. "Is everyone all right?" he asked them.

To my surprise, I saw my best friend from childhood, Lisa Miller, her father, Bruce, and her brother, Roger, all staring at us in absolute shock. "Holy crap!" I shouted. "It actually worked!" I looked down at the card which was a smoldering piece of paper. "What the heck happened to that?"

"Shelly Anderson?" the woman in her mid-twenties asked me. Lisa had dyed her hair to a perfect blond. She was still wearing expensive brand-name clothing, but the jeans were torn at the knees from sliding onto the asphalt.

I ran up and gave her a big hug. "It's so good to see you again!"

"What happened?" Her green eyes were wide as saucers. "Where are we? Dad? Roger? What's going on?"

"I don't know, Lisa—." He paused as his green eyes focused on Dad. "Timothy, is that really you?"

"It's really me. Bruce, man, it's good to see you!" He gave his old friend a bear hug. He sniffed the air around them. "Is that gunpowder?"

Bruce nodded his crew cut red hair which was now peppered with specks of gray. "I took the kids out to dinner, and someone started to shoot up the place."

The six-foot-two redhead with the build of an NFL football player gripped the handle of a metal cane as he pulled himself up. "Then this purple, swirling thing came out of nowhere and pulled us into it. The next thing we knew we ended up here. Wherever here is."

"What happened to your leg, Roger?" I asked him when I noticed the gray full-length brace over the right leg of his designer jeans.

"Car accident," he replied as he leaned on his right leg.

"You know it wasn't an accident, Roger," Lisa said.

"Why don't I take you guys to my place?" Dad suggested. "We'll talk after you guys get settled in." The Millers nodded. "Eddie, I want you to close up. Can you handle that?" There was a sudden bitter edge to his voice.

"Yes, Eddie can close up," I nearly snapped at him. "I'm coming with you guys."

Dad had driven his green Chevy Blazer to work because of the rain. We all piled into the SUV as Dad turned over the engine a couple of times before it sputtered to life. "I've missed you," Dad told Bruce who was sitting in the passenger seat. They were the only ones talking.

Bruce managed a weary smile. "Same here. How long has it been?"

"Five years."

"Everyone thought you guys died in the house fire."

Dad shook his head. "We got out just in time and then came through the same wormhole you did."

"So, where are we?" Lisa asked.

I piped up from the backseat. "Remember growing up how Robin and I would be reading all that stuff about mythology and magic? You're in an alternate reality that has magic and myth. Vampires, werewolves, wizards, unicorns, fairies, merfolk. You name it, we've probably got it. They're all real. Look, Zephyr isn't your normal city. It's a great big melting pot of myth and lore."

"What?" the Millers said at once.

"It's hard to explain, but don't worry. You'll get the hang of it," Dad said.

There was an awkward silence so I decided to break the ice. "Dad owns his own restaurant."

"Good for you, Timothy," Bruce said.

"Yeah, it's nice to run my own business," Dad said. "It beats eight-hour-long stakeouts."

Bruce only nodded. "So, what about you, Shelly? What have you been up to?"

"I'm an assistant librarian at the public library here," I said proudly. "What about you, Lisa?"

"I had my own wedding planning business. Don't know if I can start one here."

"Oh, sure you can, Lisa," I said. "Eddie's uncle is a business investor. He helped out Dad with the restaurant."

Dad pulled the car in front of his house, a white two-story ranch with four bedrooms. Dad made the Millers a quick meal of ready-to-eat lasagna and mixed vegetables and got everyone settled in. There was a knock on the front door once everyone sat down to eat. I went to open it.

"What's up with the vague text message?" my brother asked. "I just got off my shift, and I'm exhausted."

"There is someone here who wants to see you."

"Is it a hot chick?"

I smacked Robin on the back of his head, knocking his blue police cap off. "Like I would send you a text so you can meet a girl at Dad's house. This is serious."

"Ow! You just assaulted a police officer."

"I get amnesty for being your sister." I started walking down the hall. "Come on in the kitchen."

The moment we arrived, Roger got up from his seat and gave my brother a one-armed hug. "Robin, man, it's great to see you."

Robin looked from me to Dad to the Millers after Roger released him from his man hug. Crap! I hadn't told him what I done. "What is going on here?"

"Let me give you the Reader's Digest Condensed Version," I offered. "I had some dream about Lisa being in trouble, and I found a spell to open a wormhole from this reality to Pembrook."

"And it worked?" Robin asked.

"Surprisingly yes!"

My brother staggered back a bit. "Man, I've got to sit down." He plunked down into an unoccupied chair. "So, what's up?" he asked in a failed attempt to start a conversation.

Bruce took a deep breath. "The kids and I were having dinner at Panda Palace when an unmarked police car drove past and opened fire on us. Seconds later, a purple, swirling thing—like the eye of a hurricane—appeared, and we were sucked into it."

"Yeah," Lisa said as she took the last bite of her vegetables, but didn't touch the lasagna. "And the next thing we knew, we see Shelly and your dad."

"No one got hurt, did they?" Dad asked.

"Not that we know of," Bruce answered as he took a sip of his coffee.

"Did you recognize the shooter?" Dad asked.

Bruce hesitated. "No, the guy was wearing a mask."

"But you're sure he was driving an unmarked car?"

"Of course, I'm sure, Timothy," Bruce snapped. "The second I see you again, you don't believe me!"

"Well, the last time I saw you, you lied to me!"

"Hey, Roger!" Robin interrupted. "Why don't you stay with me?"

"That's a great idea," Roger replied quickly. They both said goodbye and hightailed it out of the house.

"Shelly," Dad said once the guys had left, "it's late. Why don't you and Lisa go to bed?" He glared at Bruce for a second.

"Uh, sure," I said. *So that you and Bruce can argue without us being in the room,* I thought but wisely kept it to myself. "Come on, Lisa," I said. I grabbed her hand and dragged her upstairs.

A few minutes later, I was pumping up an air mattress while she sat on my bed and combed her hair. "So, your dad really holds onto grudges?" she asked.

I stopped the hand pump and wiped the sweat from my brow. "Nah, he's just been acting strange lately."

"I mean, Dad really believed Chief Mallory was innocent of the drug charges until—." Her voice trailed off.

I heard the hesitation in her voice. "Until what?"

She lowered her voice. "Don't tell your father this. Well, I started dating James Mallory about three months ago."

"James Mallory? Is he related to the Chief of Police Thomas Mallory?"

She nodded. "James is his nephew. Dad had taken him on as a training rookie on the police force. I really liked him, but when he started constantly asking about the details on the cases Dad was working on, I realized that he was trying to get access to cases that he wasn't even assigned. Anyway, around the fifth week into our relationship, I caught him making out with his ex. After that, I dumped the jerk. But a few days later, James ransacked my apartment."

"Because you dumped him?"

She shook her head as she got up off the bed and walked to the window. "He was looking for something, I'm sure of it."

"His pride, maybe?"

She shrugged as she glanced out the window. "Ohmigod!"

"What?"

She pointed towards the window as she began to back away. "Someone is climbing up the side of the house!"

"Really?" I walked to the window and heaved it open. Lisa was right. Someone was climbing up the siding in the pouring rain. I helped him through the window. "Eddie, what are you doing?"

"You left these at the diner," the vampire said as he reached into his jean pocket. He handed me a set of keys. "I figured you might need these when your apartment isn't being fumigated anymore."

I looked at him. "You know, in my world, we had these crazy contraptions called 'doors.' I'm pretty sure that this world has them too."

Eddie ignored me. "I would've used the door, but I decided not to walk into the kitchen minefield."

"What do you mean?"

"Your dad and his friend are arguing."

Lisa gave a rather loud cough. "Oh, yeah!" I said. "Introductions. Eddie, this is one of my best friends, Lisa Miller. Lisa, this is my boyfriend, Eddie Van Helsing."

Eddie reached out to shake Lisa's hand, but she drew back hesitantly. The vampire handled it quite well by ignoring her repulsion. "Shelly's told me all about you, Lisa." He looked over at me. *Is she okay?* he asked me sublimely.

I shrugged helplessly as the vampire leaned against the wall. Lisa was probably frightened by the fact that she was in a new place. Or perhaps she thought that my boyfriend was going to bite her neck. I decided to go back to our conversation. "So, did you tell Bruce about it?"

"I did, but—." We stopped as we could hear the conversation downstairs growing louder and more intense.

"Bruce, you idiot!" Dad yelled. "Can't you keep your temper under control for once in your life?"

"I didn't know it was James until after I fired the shot. I thought he was just a burglar!"

"How could you mistake Lisa's boyfriend for a burglar? I don't think Eddie's a decent Guardian, but I would never kill him!"

I glanced over to see the vampire's expression, but his face showed nothing. When I read his mind, I had to give him credit though. He kept his thoughts on that statement G-rated.

"It was dark, Timothy," Bruce snapped. "Don't tell me that you've never done stupid things!"

"I may have, but I would never turn my back on my friend!"

"You had no physical evidence!"

"I had plenty of evidence, but you chose to ignore it!"

"You think I'm proud of that!"

"So, what did you do with the body?"

"I dumped it in a river outside of Pembrook!"

Dad sighed. "Nobody saw you?"

"Of course not, Timothy!"

"Then how come those officers took a shot at you?"

"How should I know?"

"Okay, Okay! We'll figure things out. Let's not wake the girls!"

They stopped talking, and we heard footsteps coming up the stairs. I glanced at the vampire. "Now's your time to exit!"

Eddie nodded. He turned himself into a green mist and darted underneath the window. Lisa and I watched him change back and land quietly on the lawn. He sprinted through the rain to where his motorcycle was parked.

"Shelly? Lisa?" Dad knocked on the bedroom door. "Are you guys all right?"

"Yeah, we're fine!" I said way too loudly in order to cover up the roar of Eddie's bike.

Dad hesitated. "Uh—okay then, well, good night. Shelly, are you working tomorrow?"

"Yes, I am," I replied as I glanced out the window at the vampire speeding down the street in the pouring rain. "Good night, Dad."

Once our dads went off to their separate rooms, Lisa and I quietly got ready for bed. After we finally decided that Lisa would take my bed while I slept on the air mattress, we both crawled under the covers. "So, Shelly," Lisa said quietly, "what is up with your boyfriend wearing those false fangs?"

"What do you mean?" I replied.

"Does your boyfriend thinks he's a vampire?"

"He is one."

"Oh for Pete's sake, you haven't let him bite you. Vampires are dangerous bloodsuckers.

"No, I haven't been bitten. Eddie's a vegetarian, so he doesn't drink blood."

"That's what he tells you."

"No, it's true! Both Eddie and his brother have blood allergies."

"Blood allergies?" She sounded very skeptical. "What about all the stories of vampires coming into women's rooms while they sleep and drinking their blood?"

I laughed softly. "Actually, vampires don't drink human blood. They only drink bottled animal blood. If they drink human blood, they go crazy."

"So what about Eddie? Why does he have a blood allergy?"

I shrugged in the darkness. "Don't know. Some freaky genetic thing, I guess. If he or his brother drink blood, they get really sick."

"Oh, so is Eddie supposed to be your guardian, like your dad said?"

"That I have no idea. Ever since Eddie and I started dating, Dad thinks that he wouldn't protect me."

"Why? Does Eddie protect you?"

"Yeah! Whenever I get myself in dangerous situations, Eddie's always been there for me. I don't what Dad's problem is."

"What is a guardian?"

"I have no idea, and Dad won't even tell me."

"Maybe your dad is just worried about you."

"Probably," I replied really not believing her. I decided to change the subject. "Did your dad really kill your ex?"

"It was an accident. Dad found him ransacking his house and thought he was just a common thief."

"You don't sound sorry that he died."

"James was a maggot."

"Oh! But why was he in Bruce's house?"

"I don't know, but Dad thinks it might be connected to a jewelry heist case that he just solved."

"Was James or his uncle involved?"

"I don't know." Lisa yawned. "I'm exhausted."

"Okay, we can talk later. Good night, Lisa. It's good to see you."

"Same here, Shelly."

Chapter Six:

I Make an Unpleasant Discovery at My House.

It was another boring day at the library. Mr. Folletto sulked whenever he saw me. I also could hear him mumbling under his breath that vampires should not be allowed in the library. I guess Eddie's little chat had made him pretty ticked off. The best thing was that the old elf never spoke to me, or even better, never made eye contact with me all day long. For lunch, I had a healthy salad with a bottle of water and a chocolate bar. I was feeling good.

I went home to get the shopping list I had left sitting on the table. Something was wrong the minute I stepped inside. The chemicals from the bug bomb were no longer in the air, but something was off. The bouquet of silk flowers that normally sat in the middle of the kitchen table was now lying helplessly on the floor. I carefully stepped around the glass remains of the vase. *How did this happen?* Then I remembered as I swept up the mess. I had opened the nearby window yesterday morning. I don't believe in using window screens. They're just too much trouble and look nasty when they haven't been cleaned. *The wind must have knocked it over. Or a bird must have flown in. That's just what I want: bird poop all over my house. That would make a lovely decoration.* I listened for the sound of chirping, but of course, I heard nothing. *It probably flew out*, I thought to myself. *God, I hope so.*

My bird theory flew immediately out the window when I saw the giant, silver threads hanging from the ceiling. They were about as thick as telephone lines and just as strong. One hung low enough for me to reach out and touch it. "Eew!" I said as my fingers stuck together as if they had touched super glue. I tried to shake off the sticky goo, but it would not release the death grip on my hand. I ran over to the sink and ran semi-hot water over my hand. A few minutes later, the white cotton candy substance slowly slid off and landed in the sink with a PLOP! Eddie had to see this. Maybe, he would know where it came from.

I tried to think of a way to get rid of the gunk without having it plastered to me again. Then I rummaged through my silverware drawer and pulled out a long wooden spoon. Thank God these things sell dirt cheap because Hell would freeze over before I would use the spoon again. Taking the spoon with me, I dragged a chair over to the lowest hanging thing. I stood on the chair and twisted the spoon around the mystery gunk. It stuck on the spoon like chewing gum on someone's shoe. Now, I needed something to put it in. I got down from my chair, and with my free hand, I opened the cabinet under the sink. I had several shopping bags from my latest shopping excursion stashed there. I found one with no holes and dropped in the dirty spoon. Just to be on the safe side, I tripled bagged my finding and set it on a kitchen chair.

Eddie would need to see proof of what was going on here so I went to find my camera. It was under a pile of paid bills and various piece of junk mail on my desk. I had only taken about five pictures so I had a plethora of film in my camera to take as many pictures. I took about seven different angled snapshots of the weird stuff that was taking up unnecessary space on my ceiling. I felt like some kind of abstract photographer and was treating my ceiling as if it had pieces of Rembrandt, Van Gough, or any kind of artwork other than the boring, white paint job on my ceiling.

I went back into my living room and noticed several huge gashes in the couch cushions. The closest thing to a pet that I have is my winged horse, Jordan. Something had entered my house and left those awful claws marks. My hands were trembling slightly as I took several pictures of the claw marks, especially the eight gashes on the arm next to the table where my obnoxious lava lamp was sitting. I used up the rest of the film on these particular slashes on my expensive couch. The film rewound with a little whirl. I listened intently to the camera when I suddenly heard loud scurrying coming from the loft above me. Bravery and suicide are two very different things. So, no one should blame me for deciding not to go the typical horror movie route: "Ooh, let's go into that haunted house." Three teens walk in the house. "Wait, friends, I just heard a strange noise coming from the basement. I will seal my death sentence and go check it out all by myself." I would go that route after I returned from my ski trip to Hell. I gathered up my purse, camera, and bag of white cotton candy and skedaddled out of my house.

Even Jordan seemed awfully jittery when I climbed up on her back. Maybe she could sense the evil or just plain weirdness now in my house. Frankly, the whole thing was just creeping me out. "Take me to Farley's Drug Store," I ordered Jordan. She spread her wings and within seconds, was flying high over my neighborhood.

Farley's Drug Store is owned by a satyr and his sons. It's a small mom-and-pop store nestled down the street from my house. The best thing about Farley's is their on-demand one-hour photo. The picture quality is excellent, and I would recommend it to anybody who needed photos in a hurry. That somebody happened to be yours truly. I dropped off my film and was promised to have it ready in an hour. As much as I wanted to hang out in the pharmacy, I decided instead to grab a bite to eat at the Zephyr equivalent of McDonald's. An hour later, I was paying for my perfectly developed pictures. I checked my watch. It was almost seven and almost time for Billiards Night at Anderson's place.

It was a slow Tuesday night at my dad's diner. In fact, the only customers in the restaurant were Robin and Dirk Van Helsing. The guys were surrounding a huge billiards table ready to play a game of pool. The pool table, a donation from the Count and Countess, sits off to the side near the ice cream counter. I noticed Eddie filling up a glass of strawberry cream soda for me. I walked over to the counter and took the drink from the vampire. "Thanks, Eddie."

He smiled at me. "Saw you coming. Figured you would ask for one sooner or later."

I greedily drank down about half of the soda. No excuse for acting like a pig, but I was still shaken up from my spider scare, I was entitled to act like one. I set the glass on the counter, along with the bag of the white blob and my pictures in front of a puzzled-looking Eddie. "Look what I found in my house today!" The vampire began to open the bag when I shook my head. "Use heavy-duty rubber gloves," I suggested.

Eddie fished around under the sink and produced a pair of long, green rubber gloves. He slipped them on and gingerly opened the bag as he said, "I get nervous when I'm told to open up grocery bags with gloves." The first two bags came off easily. Grabbing the wooden handle of the spoon, he grunted as he used all of his vampire strength to pull off the very last bag. Finally, it tore off with a loud RIP! Robin and Dirk both looked at us. "God, Shelly, what were you cooking?" Eddie asked as he struggled under the weight of the white junk that had now become hard as a rock.

"Very funny, Eddie!" I replied. With everyone else eavesdropping, I told my boyfriend about the white threads I found as I showed him the pictures. "I have no idea what it is. Do you?"

Dirk reached out to touch the fascinating piece of hardened goo. "Don't touch it!" I told him as if I were telling a three-year-old not to touch the good Christmas china. Eddie's brother is only a couple of years older than Eddie. He shares his brother's green eyes, and the same black hair, except that Dirk's is shoulder-length, straight, and usually pulled back in a ponytail. But Dirk is not the most graceful vampire around. He is, in fact, a walking disaster. The last time he tried his levitation spell, he broke a very expensive piece of crystal that had belonged in the Van Helsing family for a long time. "What is it, Shelly?" he asked me.

"I have no idea what it is or where it can from, Dirk," I told him. "So, I wouldn't recommend touching it."

"But Eddie gets to touch it," Dirk complained.

"Two reasons," Eddie said, "I'm her boyfriend, and I have gloves on." *Do you think it came from that spider we saw?* He asked me subliminally with a suspicious look at my findings.

God, I hope not, I told him. *Does your back still hurt from the other day?* Eddie's head shake meant that he was completely healed, physically, not emotionally. He was still shaken up from having a spider crawl on his face.

"Stop it, both of you!" Robin demanded. "I hate it when you and Eddie send telepathic messages to each other! You make weird faces."

I shrugged at my brother and turned to my boyfriend. "So, do you think you can come over to my house to survey the damages?" I asked him.

The vampire shook his head. "Maybe later, Shelly, when I'm at lunch. I don't want to leave your father and Mrs. Cross shorthanded."

I frowned. "That's okay," I said as I sat on my favorite seat at the counter, "I can wait." I looked up at the ice cream menu board. In big letters under the shakes and smoothies varieties were the words Nuclear Power Plant Smoothie. I shook my head knowing full well what every ingredient was. "Great name," I told Eddie, "I'm sure Strider will appreciate it."

"Actually, he's quite ticked off, but do I care? Not in the least bit! Want something to eat?"

I thought for a moment or two. "I'll have small, soft-serve vanilla in a cone."

"Coming up!" Eddie grabbed a cone from a cone dispenser. Then he pulled a lever on the ice cream machine, and I watched in fascination as the white ice cream poured out in a continuous swirl on top of the cone. Finally, the vampire gave it a little twist with his wrist and presented the cone with a huge curl on the tip-top.

The diner sells the best ice cream in town. Each lick was slow and satisfying as I enjoyed the cone to the fullest. "Dad should invest in rainbow sprinkles for the ice cream."

"I'll mention that to him."

"So, where is my father?"

"Giving Mr. Miller and his kids a tour of the diner. I think they're in the kitchen."

As if on cue, Dad came through the kitchen doors with Bruce, Roger, and Lisa trailing behind him. "So, Bruce, what do you think?" Dad asked him.

"It's really nice, Timothy," Bruce said shoving his hands into the pockets of what looked like new jeans. Dad must have taken them out shopping.

"I'll whip up you guys a good meal. On the house, of course. Bruce, you want to help?"

He nodded and the men left Lisa and Roger standing by themselves.

"Hey, Lisa," I said waving to her over to the ice cream counter. "I'll have Eddie serve you an ice cream. What kind of ice cream do you want?"

Lisa shook her head frantically. "No thank you."

This was not going the way I had imagined it at all. I wanted Lisa to like my boyfriend. I didn't want Lisa thinking he was supposed to be a bloodthirsty creature of the night with no heart and soul whatsoever. He wouldn't bite her even if he could. I would have to talk to her about it, alone. "Eddie, why don't you invite Roger to play a round of pool with you guys?" I asked him. *So, that I can talk to Lisa alone,* I added mentally.

He heeded my instructions and grabbed an extra cue stick. "Are we playing with no magic?" he asked the guys. The no magic rule was officially declared right after the no-Shelly rule. The last time I played with the vampire brothers and Robin, I read minds so I could anticipate their next move. Technically, it wasn't cheating. I was just getting to know my opponents. After Eddie called me out, they made the rule: Every player with a magical ability must verbally declare no use of magic. The second rule was: Shelly can not play when any member of the undead is playing. The guys all nodded, except Roger who looked confused. I hoped that Robin would explain to him what was going on. It must have been overwhelming for the Millers to come to a place where magic and myth really do exist.

"No magic?" Lisa asked me in a low voice as if she didn't want anyone to overhear her. "You're kidding me, right? Magic doesn't exist."

Maybe we should take our conversation somewhere more private. I ushered her over to a booth across the room. Lisa sat across from me. Even though I can't read the minds of the living, I knew she was skeptical. I had a feeling that she wasn't buying any of this. Time for more drastic measures. "Yeah, it does. One of the coolest things about Zephyr is when humans come here, we acquire a magical ability."

Dirk took that opportunity to slide into the seat next to me. He shot Lisa a fanged grin. "Do you want to know what my magical ability is?" he asked her. "The ability to spot a gorgeous woman."

Lisa blushed, but I turned my head away from them and made gagging noises. After I recovered, I made quick introductions. "Dirk, this is my friend Lisa Miller. Lisa, this is Eddie's brother, Dirk Van Helsing."

"As you can tell," Dirk said, "I'm the handsome one."

"Dirk," I said, "do you mind? I'm having a private conversation with a long-lost friend."

The vampire got up from the table, but never took his eyes off Lisa. He reached into the breast pocket of his green dress shirt and pulled out a business card. "Call me sometime, baby!" he said as he handed it to her. Then he walked back to the pool table.

"I can't believe I'm related to you, Dirk," Eddie said in disgust as he prepared another shot.

Lisa looked wistfully at Dirk and back at me. "You expect me to believe this magic stuff!"

I was getting frustrated. "All right, I'll prove it to you. Dad's girlfriend, Amelia can move objects with her mind."

"Oh, please!"

I ignored her comment. "I'll prove it to you." I dragged her over to where Amelia was standing behind the lectern writing something. After I made quick introductions, I asked Amelia to give us a demonstration. "Lisa's having a hard time believing in all the magic," I explained to her.

"Shelly, you know I don't like to show off my talent, but I'll do it for Lisa." Amelia turned to her. "What would you like me to move?"

Lisa pointed to a glass sitting on top of a nearby table. "Move that." I saw my friend's eyes widened in amazement as the glass lifted off the table as if being moved by invisible hands. It rose high to the ceiling, and then it whirled around one of the rafters, all without breaking. "Can I touch it?" Lisa asked.

"Sure," Amelia replied. She brought the glass back down again and let it float over to Lisa.

Lisa waved her hand over the glass as if she were looking for strings, but of course, there weren't any. She turned to face me. A look of awe was on her face. "Sorry for not believing you."

I accepted her apology with a sincere smile. "It's okay. I was the same way when we first got here."

"Can you make it go high again?"

Amelia nodded. She caused the cup to go high up into the rafters again. It perched on the edge of a cross beam. "What do you think, Lisa?"

"That is so cool! Look, Roger!"

The guys looked up from their game to where Lisa was pointing. "Why is there a glass on the rafter?" Roger asked.

"I was wondering the same thing," I heard my dad say.

We ladies turned around to see Dad and Bruce standing behind us. The tour was over, but not the fun. Amelia stepped in for our defense. "Don't worry, Honey," she assured Dad. "I won't let it break."

Just as she said that we all heard Dirk victoriously yell, "Duracell!" as a tiny purple ball of energy flew from his upraised hand to the rooftop where it, of course, hit the glass. "Should have seen that one coming," I mumbled to myself as we all watched in grim horror the cup's nosedive to death.

Dad, who was standing a good ten feet away from the falling goblet, quickly stretched out his arm and caught it mid-air. "Dirk," he said as he brought back the glass safely to Amelia's hands, "what have I told you about throwing around your spells in the diner?"

"Sorry, Mr. Anderson," Dirk apologized.

I looked over at Eddie who had smacked his forehead with the palm of his hand. Don't get me wrong. Dirk's really savvy around computers, especially the ones at the radio station where he's an overnight DJ, but he can be a klutz with his magical spells sometimes.

Bruce, Lisa, and Roger were all flabbergasted. "Timothy, what was that? Bruce asked.

"Oh," Eddie volunteered to explain, "that was my brother's war cry which also doubles as an energy spell." He looked over at Dirk. "Get another war cry, Dirk! Preferably one that doesn't have any spells connected to it."

Bruce began to back away from my dad. "What's going on here, Timothy?" he demanded. "How were you able to do that with your arm?"

Dad shrugged. "Elasticity."

"Dad, you won't believe this place," Lisa told her father, excitedly. I knew in my heart, that Lisa really believed what I had told her. "It's full of magic. Get this: Shelly's boyfriend is a real, honest-to-God vampire."

Bruce and Roger looked at me in disbelief. "A vampire?" Roger asked.

"Timothy," Bruce looked at my dad, "Is he?"

"Yep, Eddie's been working here since I opened the diner," Dad told them.

"He has a name?" Bruce asked in an almost disbelieving tone.

Boy, the Millers were definitely related. "Okay, let me make introductions," I said as Eddie walked up beside me. "Bruce, this is my boyfriend, Eddie Van Helsing. Eddie, this is Lisa's father, Bruce."

Being the kind and courteous vampire that he is, Eddie reached out to shake Bruce's hand. "Nice to meet you, sir."

Bruce made the sign of the cross. "Don't touch me!" he warned Eddie.

"Dad," Roger said, "he seems fine."

I thought now would be the time to ask Dad if Eddie could leave the diner to help me find out what was going on at my place. I quickly explained the situation to him. "So, is it all right? I mean, Lisa could stay with me once the house is cleared of whatever's in there."

"Dirk could come with us, too, Mr. Anderson," Eddie offered. "He knows a debugging spell."

"Sure," Dirk said.

Dad nodded. "Yeah, that's okay. Come back when you can." He grabbed Bruce by the shoulder and pushed him towards the kitchen.

The vampires, Lisa, and I made a quick exit out of the front door. Once we got out back, Lisa gasped in amazement the moment she saw Jordan. "What is that?" she asked.

"Oh, that's Jordan, my winged horse," I said as I untied her reins from the metal post in the employee parking area. I walked her over to where Lisa was standing. "It's okay to pet her. She won't bite."

Lisa began to stroke Jordan's muzzle. "She's so beautiful!" As she looked around, my friend nearly jumped out of her skin when she saw Tradewinds and Scotia nearby.

"Those guys belong to Dad and Amelia," I explained. "And they're both real."

"Can Jordan really fly?" she murmured in wonder.

"Sure, climb on," I said.

Lisa tried to climb onto Jordan's back, but no luck. As far as I know, my friend has never ridden a horse, much less one with wings. "I can't!"

Dirk came over to us. "Here, allow me." He squatted down and cupped his hands together. Once Lisa stepped in, he gently hoisted her up on my horse's back. "No trouble."

Eddie, not to be outdone by his brother, helped me up too. Then he leaned up and gave me a peck on the cheek. "Dirk and I will ride on my motorcycle to your place. Have a safe flight!"

"Thanks!" I said with a big, sappy grin. I watched the

vampires get on Eddie's motorcycle. Within seconds, they sped

out of the parking lot. It was time for Lisa and me to go, too.

"Lisa, hang on to me," I advised. Once she put her arms around

my waist, I instructed Jordan to take us home. Seconds later I

could hear Lisa gasping with amazement as we soared into the

night sky.

Chapter Seven:

Why Dirk Should Never be an Exterminator

I knew that Lisa really enjoyed the ride. I gave her a quick tour of

Zephyr as Jordan took us over rooftops of homes and office

buildings. She gawked in amazement as we flew by an elf riding

a dragon that was about the size of Jordan. Finally, we landed right in front of my house where the guys were waiting for us. As soon as I put Jordan away in her little stable that was about the size of a shed, I walked over to where Lisa was standing with the vampires who were peering into the kitchen windows. I apparently had left the light on when I left in a hurry.

"Holy cow, Shelly!" Eddie said. "That's a lot of cobwebs! I can barely see your sink."

I muscled my way to the window and looked into a winter-like wonderland. "Oh, crap!" I moaned as I unlocked my door. It would take me forever to clean up this mess. I tried to open the door, but it held fast. I tried jiggling the lock, but still, it wouldn't budge. Maybe I just thought I had unlocked it. No, that wasn't it because I could still turn the doorknob. I glanced over at Eddie and Dirk. "A little help here, guys!"

"What seems to be the problem?" Eddie asked me.

"I can't open my door!"

Eddie had me step aside. He grabbed the doorknob and pressed against it with his vampire strength. A few seconds later, the door popped open to reveal a cave-like path lined with the white, thread-like goo in my kitchen. "This is disgusting, Shelly."

"What is it?" Lisa asked.

For the first time, I didn't have an answer for her. I began to wonder if Dirk's spell could really clear out every one of these cobwebs. "So," I asked him, "can you pull off this spell?"

"Of course, I can!" Dirk replied confidently. He rolled up the arms of his shirt. "Stand back!" When we were a good five feet behind him, he asked me if I wanted the entire house debugged.

"No, I just want the kitchen cleared," I sarcastically answered his idiotic question. "Of course, I want the whole house debugged!"

"Your wish is my command!" Dirk drew in a deep breath to prepare for the spell. "Pesticide house!" he shouted with a voice of command as he lifted up his hands. A green, swirling wind escaped from his palms and swept up all the cobwebs in its path making them disappear to a tar pit about a thousand miles away. When the wind had cleaned up the last cobweb, the vampire closed his fists, taking the wind back from whence he had summoned it. He turned to me with a satisfactory smile on his face. "Now, your house is bug-free!" the wanna-be exterminator informed.

Lisa and I stepped inside. Dirk had not screwed up the spell this time. "Thanks, guys," I told them. I waved good-bye to the vampires as they headed back to Eddie's motorcycle. I shut the door behind us.

Lisa was looking around at my kitchen. "Nice place," she said.

I gave her a tour of my house. Finally, we ended up back in the kitchen. "Do you want anything to eat?" I offered as I looked in the pantry for something quick to make.

"Sure, what do you have?"

I pulled out a box of garden herb Ready Rice and a can of peas. "Sorry, I don't have any meat."

"That's okay, Shelly. I'm vegan."

"Oh!" That explained why she never touched the lasagna or the ice cream.

With Lisa's help, the meal was done in about thirty minutes. "So, how long have you been dating Eddie?"

"We just started dating, but he's been one of my best friends for a couple of years. I really like Eddie. He's kind and considerate. He's everything and more than I've ever wanted in a boyfriend."

Lisa smiled. "He seems wonderful like his brother." Then she seemed to remember something. "Shelly, at the diner, you were telling about the various magical abilities that your dad, his girlfriend, and Robin have, but you never told me yours. Do you have one?"

"I'm telepathic."

"Really? So, you can read my mind?"

"Unfortunately, no! I have limited telepathy." She seemed surprised at my statement so I explained, "I can only read the minds of the undead."

"Like vampires and werewolves?"

I nodded. "The mind of both vampires and werewolves are fairly easy to read, except that vampires can block mind reading. Ghosts' minds are a little harder to read because they tend to wander from place to place."

"Why is that a problem?"

"I can only read minds if they are in the same room with me. Something about the physical barriers, I think. Zombies are the hardest to read because their brains mostly rot out in the grave."

"So, do you send Eddie telepathic messages?"

"Lots of times!" I said with a smile. "Robin hates it when we do that, especially when we're making fun of him." I saw Lisa rubbing her eyes and yawning. "You look exhausted, Lisa. Why don't you go to bed? I have tomorrow off so I can show you around." I showed her where she would be sleeping and lent her an old tee-shirt and ratty pair of sweatpants to sleep in. It took me an hour or so, but I finally drifted off into a dreamless sleep.

The rapid knocking on my wall awakened me out of a deep sleep. I rolled over to look at the digital clock on my nightstand. Two-thirty in the morning? The pounding continued. "Shelly?" I heard coming from the other side of the wall. I remembered Lisa was sleeping in my guest room which was right next to my bedroom. Was sleeping! Something woke her up. I rolled out of bed and pressed my ear against the wall.

"Lisa," I asked, "what's wrong?"

"Listen!" I could hear the apprehension in her voice, "I think there is someone or something in the living room."

Lisa was right. I tuned my ears to the faint rustling sounds that were coming somewhere beyond my door. I tiptoed over to the door and dropped to the floor to peer underneath it. I held back a gasp as I saw something move back and forth in the shadows cast by the lava lamp in the living room. Pulling myself to my feet, I began to gather up my courage. I opened the door about three inches and screamed in horror at what I saw. A normal, brightly colored spider was running back and forth across the living room. If you could call a spider the size of a Saint Bernard normal. It saw me and ran for the door at full speed on all of its eight legs. I slammed the door tight just as the spider rammed into it, nearly knocking the door off the hinges. The thing must have scurried back to the kitchen. I had an idea, but Lisa would have to get to my room. Quickly, I slipped on a pair of jeans, a rumpled light pink long-sleeved tee, and my good, old, reliable sneakers.

"Shelly," Lisa asked through the wall, "what's out there?"

I pressed my ear up to the wall. "Lisa, you still afraid of spiders?" I asked.

"Yes! Why? What's going on?"

"Okay, I want you to put away all of your fears for a few moments. All right?" Yeah, Shelly, there you go. Tell the arachnophobe to ignore the giant spider in your living room. "Get dressed. I'm going to open my door. When I yell for you, I want you to run into my bedroom as fast as you can."

"Okay, but what is going on? What is out there?"

You don't want to know, I thought to myself. I slowly opened the door as quietly as a mouse. The thing was nowhere in sight, which was a good thing. "Now, Lisa!" I yelled as I swung open the door.

The guest bedroom flung open and Lisa began to run to my room when the spider-thing came into view. My friend screamed the moment she saw it and froze in place. The thing looked upon her with all its millions of beady evil eyes but stood still like a statue. It was like a gun duel in those old Western movies, but with a spider the same size as Cujo.

"Lisa, get in here!" I yelled, shaking her out of the trance. "Do something! Yell! Scare it!"

"Shoo!" she yelled. Bolts of red and white light shot out from the palms of her hands. The thing squealed in pain as it shrank back away from her. Somehow, she must have temporarily blinded it. Unfortunately, Lisa didn't move. She just stood there, staring down at her hands in absolute surprise.

I finally ventured out into the living room and yanked the stunned Lisa into my bedroom, slamming the door behind us. The spider must have regained its sight because it attempted to battle-ram my door. Oh, yeah! I was going to need a new door before the night was up.

"W-W-What? H-H-How did—?" Lisa stammered, still staring down at her hands.

"The light coming out of your hands?" I said as I picked my cell phone off the nightstand and hit the speed dial button reserved for my boyfriend's cell number. "I'm guessing that it might be your magical ability, but we can ask Eddie about it." I could hear it ringing. At least, he had it on. "Come on, Eddie! Pick up, pick up the freaking phone!" I mumbled to myself.

"Hello?"

I gave a huge sigh of relief when I heard the vampire's voice. "Eddie, it's me, Shelly. Can you come over to my place, like right now?"

"I thought you were waiting 'till marriage."

"Get your mind out of the gutter, Eddie Van Helsing!" I shouted at the phone. "Come to my bedroom window when you get here."

"Tempting, but—."

I cut him off. "Lisa and I are trapped in my bedroom because there's a giant spider taking up residence in my living room!" The spider slammed against the door again. "And if you don't get your rear in gear, we might be crushed by the weight of the door when it breaks down!"

"Oh!" Eddie sounded shocked. "Just how big is this spider?"

Lisa and I exchanged nervous glances as the door trembled again. "I'm taking a long shot," I told the vampire, "but I would say about the size of your motorcycle. Wouldn't you say that's about right, Lisa?"

Lisa shook her head. "Oh, no! It's bigger, much bigger!"

"I'm on my way, Shelly," Eddie assured me as I heard him climb into one of his cars. "Hang on!" He hung up his phone leaving Lisa and me to listen to the destructive noises caused by the thing right out of a B-horror film in my living room.

We jumped the second the rock hit the windowpane in my bedroom. I drew back the curtain to see my boyfriend looking around for another rock to throw. I heaved the window open, and he leaped in through the window where he landed a few feet in front of Lisa and me. Eddie looked down at my disheveled outfit with concern. "Please, tell me you don't sleep in your clothes," he told me.

"No!" I snapped back. "Can you get us out of here?"

He nodded. "But first, I want to see what we're dealing with." He changed himself into a green mist, and as if he were being propelled by a breeze, the vampire slipped under the bedroom door. "I don't see anything, Shell," he called from the other side of the door. Suddenly, we heard a shout of surprise. The green midst darted back under the door just as the spider ran up against it. A hinge popped out, falling to the floor. Eddie materialized in front of us. "Get out now!"

Lisa began to climb through the window as Eddie grabbed her hand and helped her down safely. Then it was my turn. I paused for a moment to look over my shoulder as the door broke down. The spider was running straight at me. I lost all my courage the moment I realized that the thing was about the size of a pony and probably weighed the same, too. All my muscles suddenly refused to cooperate with each other, and I couldn't force myself to move.

Eddie leaped up in mid-air and threw his arms around my waist. Not very romantic under the circumstances. Then he pulled me out the window, banging my knee on the window sill in the process. He set me down on the ground, but still clutched my hand as the three of us ran to the carrot car. Lisa flew open the side door and dove in across the back seat where Dirk was waiting in the back.

I glanced over my shoulder as I skidded to a stop. I stood in the damp grass and heard the shattering of glass coming from my bedroom. The gigantic spider had taken out the entire window and about three feet of wood and siding that was around the window with it. Eddie yanked on my arm and just about dragged me to the car where I stumbled into the passenger seat.

Eddie slammed the door shut and leaped over the car. Quickly, he changed into mist and slid between the cracks of the driver's side door. He materialized behind the steering wheel. Being the smart guy that he is, Eddie had left the keys in the ignition. He started the car and peeled out of the driveway. "You all right, Shelly?" he asked me as soon as we were on the road. "You kind of froze there for a moment."

"You-you-you would, too," I stammered as I tried to steady my shaking hands, "if you saw a spider take out both your bedroom door and a window."

Eddie gave my hand a gentle squeeze. "I've seen a lot worse than that," he said. Even though the statement was sincere, it didn't do anything for my nerves. He glanced up in the rearview mirror. "How are you holding up, Lisa?"

"Fine, fine," she replied, nervously. She suddenly noticed Dirk by her side. "Hi!" she said to him. "What was that thing?"

Dirk shrugged. "I honestly don't have a clue, but I'm sure we'll find out." He glanced out the back window. "For Pete sakes, Eddie!" He began to hyperventilate. "Drive! Drive! Drive!"

"I'm going as fast as I can!" Eddie snapped back.

"It's gaining on us, Eddie!"

"I'm well aware of that, Dirk!"

We all glanced behind us. The spider which had doubled in size was galloping toward us. "Can you outrun this thing?" I asked Eddie in a low voice.

"I can outrun anything." Eddie checked his side mirror. I guess objects in mirrors are closer than they appear because my boyfriend hit the accelerator hard as he shifted gears "Hang on!"

The ground shook the car back and forth as if it were body surfing in a mosh pit. Lisa glanced out the back window. "It's following us!" she shrieked as a bright purple light flared from her hands.

Eddie and Dirk both winced in pain as they momentarily shut their eyes. Things were going just great. *My house is in shambles,* I thought. *My long-lost best friend nearly blinds and deafens Dirk and Eddie who is traveling well over the posted speed limit.* To top it off, we were now being chased by a spider on steroids. Could this night get any worse?

Suddenly the car was tilted up on its right side. Super! The spider was checking the car for mechanical problems. My head came in contact with the passenger window. Then I felt a small WHUMP as my boyfriend slammed into me. He apparently wasn't wearing his seat belt. "Lisa, Dirk, are you guys all right?" I asked, not bothering to find out if Eddie was all right. Vampires are really fast healers.

"I just hit my head," Lisa said. She put her hand to the side of her head.

Dirk sniffed the air. "You're not bleeding that bad, Lisa," he told her. He knew what she was thinking by the sudden intake of air. "All vampires can smell the slightest drop of blood. I just can't drink it," he explained to her. He reached into the pocket of his jeans and pulled out a handkerchief. "This should slow the bleeding, Lisa."

Eddie's brow furrowed in thought. I jumped into his mind to see what he was thinking. "Have you lost your freaking mind?" I demanded of him.

"Look, do you want us to get out of here alive?"

I nodded.

"I thought so." Eddie glanced at his brother. "Come on, Dirk!"

Dirk frantically shook his head. "Why don't I stay in the car to protect the girls?"

Eddie rolled his eyes and muttered, "Wuss." He glanced at me. "I'll be okay. Just push me up towards my door," he told me firmly as he attempted to crawl up the vinyl bench seat.

I placed my hands on his sexy tush and gave him a hard shove. This was probably the only time I would get a chance to touch him there, and it wasn't even close to a romantic situation!

Why couldn't he climb up the ceiling using his vampire senses?

"Can you move any faster?"

"I'm trying!" Eddie protested. He reached up to grab the door handle and pulled himself up forward. He turned himself into mist and slid through the crack under the door.

It was just Lisa, Dirk, and me inside the car. She wiped away the last remaining blood from her head as she said, "I bet you enjoyed getting your hands on his butt."

I smiled. "Tell me about it."

"Why didn't you help your brother?" Lisa asked Dirk.

"I can more easily protect you in here than I can out there."

I rolled my eyes at Dirk. Unlike his brave brother, Dirk is a wimp when comes to dangerous situations.

Lisa looked out the back window. The spider thing was still holding up the car. We could hear one of its legs scraping against the carriage of the car. Then we heard my boyfriend's footsteps as he walked across the side of the car. "What is he doing?" Lisa asked me.

"He's going to see if his energy spell will knock away the spider thingy," I replied just as we heard Eddie shout the word "DURACELL!" We all watched through the side windows as a huge ball of blue energy shot across the sky. We placed our hands over our ears as the spider unleashed an unearthly scream. The car fell back to earth with a hard thump, almost giving us whiplash.

Seconds later, a green mist appeared in the car. Eddie materialized back in his seat. He floored the accelerator. "You guys all right?" he asked in a hoarse voice. The spell had taken a lot from him.

"We're fine. You?" I asked, noticing the vampire's trembling hands and heavy breathing.

"Just tired. You got someplace to stay for the night?"

"As much as I want to sleep in a room with a huge hole open to the elements, the answer is no." I raised an eyebrow. "Why, is this an invitation?"

Chapter Eight:
When a Spider Is Not Really a Spider

The three-minute drive to the Van Helsing house was fairly quiet. Eddie expertly maneuvered the high speeding car into its designated parking spot in the garage and closed the door behind us.

Lisa and I followed the guys into their house through the back door which led right into the kitchen. We made ourselves at home sitting upon two of the wooden bar stools in front of the huge black island counter. "You want something to drink?" Eddie asked as he poured himself a huge mug of fresh pineapple juice. He drank half of it before listing off the huge variety of drinks in the fridge.

"I'll have a glass of fruit punch, Eddie," I told my boyfriend as I rested my head in my hands. "You, Lisa?" I asked my friend.

Lisa gave me a cautious look and then asked for a glass of lemonade. Eddie poured my fruit juice for me while Dirk decided to be a gentleman and got Lisa a tall glass of lemonade. I was beginning to think he was developing a crush on my friend. Dirk saw the dried up blood on Lisa's head. He came up behind her and gently touched her wound. "Penicillin," he whispered as the cut immediately healed up.

"What did you do?" Lisa asked him.

"Your cut's all healed," Dirk said as he crossed his arms. "I used a healing spell on your cut. It only heals minor injuries. Actually, I'm quite well known among the ladies as 'Doctor Dirk.'"

My fruit punch almost spilled from out of my nose when I heard Dirk's world-famous pick-up line. Doctor Dirk? Usually, it was followed by, "And can I call you, 'Nurse (insert the name of the woman the vampire was hitting on)?'" He even tried to use it on me when I first met him. Lame, I know. I'm so thankful that Eddie has never used any awful pick-up lines on me when we first met. I would probably slap him silly if he ever pulled one on me. "Want to explain to me why your debugging spell didn't work?" I asked.

Dirk scowled at me because I had shut down his Cassanova act. "It did work, but obviously this is no ordinary spider. Don't you think you're overreacting just a little bit, Shelly?"

So, help me, God, if there weren't a four-foot wide counter top between us, I would have flown across and strangled my boyfriend's brother. As if I weren't under enough stress already, Dirk's little comment had pushed me over the edge, and there was no way of regaining my sanity. "No, I am not overreacting!" I exploded. "I have absolutely no privacy in my bedroom because the door is in pieces on the floor! And I'm screwed if someone wants to walk through the mac-truck size hole in my wall and rob me! Did you see the same gigantic spider that I did? Then, I think I'm entitled to overreact!"

Everyone's jaws were agape in utter shock. I must've looked like I belonged in a straitjacket. Lisa finally spoke in a soft voice, "Shelly, your door can be fixed."

"It's not that!" I said, trying to keep my temper from flaring up again. "It's this freaking spider! I can't get rid of it! I'm not even sure if the thing is really a spider."

Eddie looked at me funny. He needed to know all about the spider thing in order to find out what it was. "Shelly," he said as he placed his hand on my trembling hand, "why don't you tell us from the beginning how the spider got in your house in the first place?"

I told them everything about the book and the spider dropping out of it, the growing cobwebs, and the invincible spider. They heard every stinking detail. By the time I was done with my long saga, I was on my third glass of fruit punch. "So, what is it?" I finally asked Eddie and Dirk.

"Are you thinking what I'm thinking?" Dirk asked his brother.

Eddie nodded grimly. The look on their faces scared me. It's a disturbing sign when vampires get worried.

"What are you thinking?" Lisa asked them. Then she turned to me for information. "What's going on, Shelly?" She had been informed that her best friend could read the minds of the undead.

I drifted into Dirk's mind first. He was trying to remember details about some kind of creature that lurks in books. Then I traveled into his brother's mind. There were only two words racing back and forth in Eddie's mind. "Eddie, what's a book demon?" I asked in an uncertain voice.

"Uh," he started to say, unable to get over the fact that his girlfriend had this book demon terrorizing her. He glanced over to Dirk for some help.

Dirk gave it. "A book demon is a type of demon that Welkies like to place in books."

"What's a Welkie?" Lisa asked. She was new here in Zephyr, and I hadn't explained to her about the magical race of the Welkie.

"It's a race of humans who possess a vast amount of magic," Dirk said in another effort to impress Lisa. "Welkies can live on for centuries." He realized that Lisa had no idea what he was talking about. "Welkies can perform any kind of magical spells."

"They're essentially known as wizards, sorcerers, enchantresses, and witches," I volunteered as Eddie washed our glasses.

"What's the difference between them?" Lisa asked.

Dirk decided to answer her. "The way they use their magic. If they use it for good causes, we call them wizards and if they're female Welkies, enchantresses,"

"If they use their magic for bad, then they are known as sorcerers and witches," Eddie said the last two words as if he were spitting something bad out from his mouth. I wish I knew why he hates sorcerers. But whenever I try to read his mind to find out the answer, he always blocks out my attempts.

I glanced over at Lisa who had a confused look on her face. "Think of Welkies as the X-Men and the Brotherhood of Evil Mutants," I offered. Now that we had explained to Lisa what Welkies are, I wanted to get back to my big problem. "Can we get back to the problem at hand?" I asked. "What is a book demon, and how am I going to get rid of it?"

Eddie sighed at my impatience. "Well, demons are classified at five levels."

"How so?" I asked.

"By physical characteristics and intelligence," Dirk replied.

Eddie understood my puzzled look. "The more humanoid they look, the more intelligent and sometimes dangerous they are."

"But Shelly's demon is a spider," Lisa pointed out.

"Book demons aren't usually dangerous, and they aren't that intelligent. They are mostly Level One demons."

"What do you mean by 'mostly,' Eddie?" I asked. I had a feeling that I wasn't going to like the answer.

"It depends on the type of book they are in." He paused as he remembered to ask me something very pertinent. "Shelly, what was the name of that book again?"

"Something like *Wild and Wacky Weather,* if I remember correctly. It was a book on natural disasters."

Both Dirk and Eddie gave involuntary gasps as if I had just announced that I was joining a convent. As I found out by reading their minds, the genre of the book determines the demon's actions. Now, I know why my house and life were turned upside down. "Shelly, did you notice if the book was unusually heavy?" Dirk asked.

What a dumb question to ask a librarian. "I deal with about a hundred books on a daily basis for five days a week! How am I supposed to tell whether a book is unusually heavy or not?" I countered.

"Wait, can we get back to the demon thing?" Lisa asked. "I want to know more about them." She looked at Dirk as if he knew all about demons. In fact, it was Eddie who seemed to know more about them. "So, Dirk, do these book demons always take on the forms of spiders?"

Dirk shook his head. "No, usually the Welkie who put the demon inside the book decides what form the demon will take."

"Then how come I didn't see the demon when I was looking at the book at the yard sale?" I asked.

Eddie answered my question for me. "With your case, it sounds like it was invisible while it was inside the book. Once you dropped the book, the demon fell out, becoming visible."

"So, this is nice and everything, but the real question is: How do we get rid of this thing?" I didn't like the look on the vampires' faces, and I didn't like the answer that was in their minds either. "What do you mean you don't know?" I asked them.

"Shelly, it depends on the Welkie," Eddie said in a fruitless attempt to calm me down. "They know how to get rid of the demon that they created. So, you're going to have to talk to the Welkie who put it in the book. What I do know about book demons is once you get them back inside the book they came in, you have to destroy the book, and the demon will die as well. "

I sighed as I leaned back in my chair. My boyfriend was right about me having to talk to the Welkie. I was the one who unleashed this book demon. "Super! Just super!" I complained. So, now it was my responsibility to find out how to get rid of it. Not even Eddie's powerful fire spells could even hurt it, and to top it all, I had no idea what to do. "Okay, I'll do it tomorrow afternoon," I said as I rubbed my tired eyes.

Eddie showed us two of their guest rooms. Lisa's room was like mine with a king-size bed and its own bathroom suite.

The color of her silk satin sheets was hunter green while the color in my room was purple. Staying in one of the guest rooms at the Van Helsing mansion is almost like staying in the penthouse suite at the Ritz Carlton.

I changed into an old t-shirt that Eddie lent me to sleep in and collapsed in the mountain of pillows. I lay awake for a long time, thinking about everything that had transpired in the past few hours. A wave of paranoia swept over me. What if the book demon came here and destroyed the house? Or even worse, killed us all? Then I realized how safe we were. The guys have a protective spell over the house and everyone in it. Nothing magical could harm me while I was inside. "Oh my gosh! Jordan's still at the house!" I said aloud as I sat straight up in bed. I had completely forgotten about my winged horse. What if the book demon had attacked her? I jumped out of bed and threw on my jeans and shoes. I slipped out of the room and went to find Eddie.

Music was blaring from a radio sitting on a sawhorse near the picklemobile in the huge garage. I could hear Eddie belting out the words, "I wanna rock and roll all nite and party every day!" I followed the sound of his voice to where the picklemobile was propped up on cement blocks about three feet off the concrete floor.

"Gene Simmons, you ain't," I said, announcing my presence.

The vampire slid out from under the car on a piece of plywood on wheels. "Hey, Shelly!" he said. "What are you doing up?" He pulled himself to an upright seated position.

"You've some oil on your cheek. No, the other one." I said as Eddie wiped the oil off with a handkerchief. I sat crosslegged on the floor next to him. "I couldn't sleep," I admitted. "I'm really worried about Jordan. We left her there alone with that thing. Do you think that we could—?"

Eddie shook his head. "I'm not going out again and put you in danger with that demon running around." He put an arm around me. "Shelly, Jordan's a smart horse. I'll bet she flew away. I'm sure she's all right."

I sighed. He was right. Jordan wasn't stupid enough to

hang around when there's a spider thingy that's really a demon

running loose. "But I just can't forget about her, Eddie!"

"Look, I know how much she means to you, but I don't

want you wandering around town with that demon still at large.

It's too dangerous."

I let that sink in for a while as I listened to the radio blaring

out to another song. I knew that the vampire was really

concerned about my safety. Thinking that our conversation was

over, Eddie had slid back under the car. "So, how did it go back

at the diner?" I asked him.

"Oh, just peachy," Eddie replied. "Mr. Miller was really

getting on my nerves when I got back. He demanded to know

where I had taken you and Lisa, accusing me of draining your

blood. Other than that, it went great." If I had x-ray vision, I could

probably see the smirk on my boyfriend's face.

"Well, they have been through a lot lately," I replied. I was

about to tell him Lisa's story, but then I decided against it. What

Lisa had told me was most likely in confidence. I scrambled to

my feet as I realized that I was nodding off. Even though I had a busy and frightening night, exhaustion swept over me like a tidal wave. "I'm going back to bed. Good night, Eddie,"

"Good night, Shell," Eddie replied from under the car. He slid back out and pulled himself upright. He gave me a kiss on the cheek. "You're exhausted. Get some sleep."

Chapter Nine:
She's Gone Mad! Stark Raving Mad!

Lisa was sitting at the counter when I wandered into the kitchen. She had a big bowl of Fruitos in front of her. She was still wearing the clothes from last night. "Want some breakfast?" she asked me.

"I see you found your way around their kitchen," I said as I opened the fridge to get out the milk jug. I grabbed a bowl from one of the cupboards. Then, I went to the pantry. Since when does Eddie eat Fruitos? They taste exactly like cardboard. "You like that cereal?" I asked Lisa as I poured myself a bowl of Honey Rings.

"It was sitting on the counter when I came down this morning," Lisa replied.

I nodded. Dirk must have bought the cereal for her. He wouldn't give up. Persistent little twit. Lisa didn't need to know that Dirk was hitting on her. Not yet anyway. I poured the milk into my cereal and sat down beside my friend. "I was thinking that we could go talk to the guy who sold me the book, and then I can you show around town."

"That'll be interesting," Lisa said as she got up to rinse her bowl. What else could she say? "I guess I'll go get ready for the day. Oh, by the way, your boyfriend left you a package." She jerked her head towards the kitchen table where a plastic bag was sitting on one of the placemats.

As soon as Lisa went to shower, I opened the bag to discover two bottles of my favorite shampoo and conditioner. A note fell out, and I picked it up and read it aloud. "'Shelly, I hope this is the same stuff you use for your hair. Talk to you later. Love, Eddie.'" I smiled. He was so thoughtful and very observant. Not even my closest girlfriends knew what kind of shampoo and conditioner I used. I finished up my cereal, grabbed the bag and went off to get ready for the day.

Within an hour, Lisa and I were both ready to go for the day. We were still wearing our clothes from last night. I decided I would take Lisa shopping after we talked to the werewolf who sold me the book. We started to leave when I remembered that we needed some form of transportation. Jordan probably wasn't here anyway. She will only fly here if instructed. "I need to ask Eddie something," I told Lisa.

"Won't he die if you open his coffin?" Lisa asked me as we walked up the stairs to the second floor. The "bedroom floor," as I call it, splits off into three hallways with about four rooms per section. We walked down the middle hallway to the second door on the left.

"No," I laughed as I knocked on Eddie's bedroom door. "Vampires don't sleep in coffins like they do in the movies. They sleep in regular beds."

"Who is it?" a groggy voice came from the other side.

"It's Shelly, Eddie," I said. "Can we borrow one of your cars?"

There was a soft thump and shuffling across the bedroom's hardwood floor. The door opened halfway. Eddie leaned against the doorframe, wearing only a pair of blue and white plaid drawstring pants.

I gave a gasp as I gazed momentarily at the vampire's hunky bare chest. Boy, was he sexy or what? Of course, this wasn't the first time I had seen Eddie bare-chested, and it still looked great. "I-we-need-can we borrow one of your cars?"

He nodded. "Which one do you want?" he asked.

"How about the picklemobile?" I asked.

"Let me get the keys for you," Eddie replied. He turned around and shuffled to where a wooden key rack hung over the bed. He picked up a ring with two keys on it and tossed them to me. "Be careful with the car," he told me. He knew I was a good driver, but he just cared a lot about the green piece of junk. He gave me a kiss on the cheek. "I'll see you guys tonight at the diner."

We thanked him and shut the door behind us. Once we were in the car and had pulled out of the driveway, Lisa asked the question that must have been bugging her ever since we saw Eddie this morning. "So, Shelly, how many times has Eddie kissed you?"

I felt the heat rush to my cheeks. Go away, blush, go away. "Five times, I think." I stared ahead watching out for any sign of Jordan or the demon. Maybe it was nocturnal and would only come out at night. Yeah, right. Maybe I can sell that oceanfront property in Arizona while I'm at it.

"You really like him, don't you?"

I nodded as we drove towards Wildflower Street. "Eddie's a great guy. I think he's the one." My eyes widened in surprise as we noticed the damage. Piles of trash were scattered all over the road. I swerved to miss a piece of siding that had come off an abandoned house nearby. It looked like something had stepped on the house itself and squashed it flat. Similar houses were badly damaged with gaping holes where windows and roofs should have been. I saw some people sitting away from their damaged property wailing. while others comforted them. The only thing I can compare the damage to is the media pictures of hurricanes or tornadoes' aftermath. What had I released? Finally, we pulled into the driveway of Norton Wolfbane. With Lisa right behind me, I bounded up the two front steps and pressed the doorbell once.

"Mr. Wolfbane!" I blurted out when the werewolf opened the door for us. "What happened here?" I pointed to the destruction all over the street.

"A giant spider destroyed all of my neighbors' properties," Mr. Wolfbane said as he ushered us inside his home. "I can't believe what this neighborhood is coming." He looked at us, me especially as if he didn't recognize me. Of course, I had bought the stupid book from him a few weeks ago, and I had just barged into his home. "Do I know you?" he asked me.

"I'm Shelly Anderson. I came to your yard sale. I was with the pregnant fairy, the one who you sold the bassinet to."

"Ah, yes," he replied as his grey eyes lit up with recognition, "you were the one who bought that book on natural disasters." He gestured to the two wicker chairs that sat on the front porch. I wondered how his house could have survived the demon's destruction. By reading his mind, I realized that Mr. Wolfbane had used his camouflage spell to hide his house. Smart man. "Let me go get you, ladies, some tea." He came back out with a white plastic tray loaded with a steaming teapot and two teacups.

"Yeah," I replied as Lisa and I graciously accepted his offer for some tea. "I was kind of wondering where you got that book." I seated myself and took a sip of my strawberry tea.

"Well," the werewolf replied, "an elderly wizard friend of mine gave to it me about twenty years ago."

"Did he put some kind of spell on it?" I asked.

"Not that I'm aware of. Why do you ask, Miss Anderson?"

I gave him a Reader's Digest Condensed version of what had happened in the last few days. "My boyfriend thinks it might be some kind of book demon that was hiding inside the book," I finished up with my story.

The wolfman gave a short gasp. "Oh, my! Willard did mention about putting something inside the book when he gave it to me." Apparently, this Willard guy was the Welkie that we're looking for. "Willard Houdini was a prankster of a wizard. He liked to put surprises in different objects, mostly harmless demons though. I remember him telling me one time his demons grow if they are exposed to colored lights. Unfortunately, that's all he told me about them."

The annoying lava lamp that hopefully was still sitting on the end table in my living room flashed across my mind. So, that's how the demon thing grew. I remembered the first time Lisa used her light powers. That thing probably grew without us realizing it, but Mr. Wolfbane was holding something back about this wizard, and I needed to find out what. "Do you have Mr. Houdini's contact information? I really need to talk with him," I must have sounded pretty desperate to the werewolf.

Mr. Wolfbane shook his head sadly. Before I had a chance to read his mind, he told us why. "Mr. Houdini has been dead for about ten years. Blew himself up, the poor soul"

Terrific! I thought to myself. My week was going to Hell in a handbasket. It just reached Hell's sixth layer. Lisa and I thanked Mr. Wolfbane for everything as we left his house.

"Now what?" Lisa asked me the second I slammed the driver's side door.

I buckled up my seat belt. "I have no idea," I said as I laid my head back. Then I had a bright idea. "Maybe if we go shopping, I can attempt to figure out what to do." Lisa agreed. For the next couple of hours, we spent shopping at the twenty-four-hour Moonlight Mall for some new clothes for Lisa.

Around noon, I called Robin to ask if he and Roger (who was staying with him) could pick up a couple of huge pieces of plywood, some nails, and a couple of hammers and meet us at my house in two hours. Robin didn't ask me why.

Even as I told the guys what happened while they put plywood over my window, they had a hard time believing that I had unleashed a book demon. We promised to meet them back at the diner at six. For the rest of the afternoon, Lisa helped me cleaned up the mess in my kitchen.

When we arrived at Anderson's Place, I parked besides Eddie's motorcycle. Lisa and I got out and walked through the back doors. We noticed there were absolutely no customers in the diner. We saw my dad and Bruce crowded around a radio that was sitting on the ice cream counter. Eddie was sipping a glass of cola at the other end of the counter. I waved to him and got the subliminal message that he sent me. He hadn't mentioned to Dad or Bruce that Lisa and I had slept at his house. Dad wouldn't have cared. It was Bruce's reaction that I was worried about. "Hi, Dad! Hi, Bruce!" I said as we walked over to them. "What's going on? Why is there no one in here?" I asked.

"The city placed a mandatory curfew 'cause of some giant spider running around and destroying property all over," Dad explained to us.

Just then we heard a familiar voice on the radio. "Good evening, folks! This is Dirk Van Helsing on KZRR. The mayor has given an order asking everyone to stay inside because of a dangerous giant spider running rampant in the streets. Now, back to more of your favorite rock 'n roll classics!" A song filtered through the radio.

Dad turned down the volume. "Apparently, this thing has smashed an abandoned apartment building, torn off the roof of a nearby bar, and threw a couple of dumpsters at some people who are now in the hospital among other things," he told us.

I glanced over at Eddie who was about to mention the book. I shook my head at him. *Don't say anything!* I sent the telepathic message with determination in my mind. Eddie didn't know much about the demon, and the last thing we needed was everyone to panic before I told them what I had learned. *I need to talk with you in the kitchen, Eddie. Now!* I excused myself and headed toward the kitchen. "I'm going to get something to drink!" I announced over my shoulder.

"Let me help you out, Shelly," Eddie said. He followed me into the kitchen while Bruce shot a dirty look at him. The second we were out of everyone's earshot and under the cover of the hum of the dishwasher, I was distracted for a moment, realizing I hadn't seen my dad's girlfriend around. "Where's Amelia?" I asked Eddie.

"She called in sick today," Eddie said. He wanted to get back to the subject at hand. "So, what did you find out about the demon?" he asked softly.

"Okay, Lisa and I went to Mr. Wolfbane's home—his neighborhood was a mess, Eddie." I shuddered at the thought of the demon rampaging throughout the city. "Anyway, he said that the wizard who put the demon inside the book was a bit of a prankster. Supposedly, the demons were always harmless."

"That's all well and good, Shell, but did you talk to the wizard?"

"Nope, but we can go right over to the cemetery and have a little chit-chat with his tombstone."

Eddie ran his fingers through his curly hair. "Is that all you found out?" he demanded a bit more loudly. "So, how do we get rid of it?"

"I don't know."

"How come you don't know?"

"Because he didn't tell me!"

"Couldn't you read his mind?"

"I did, but that was all he knew!" I couldn't believe that my voice was raising a couple of octaves.

"Shelly, you unleashed this thing, and now you've got to get rid of it!"

Just then Dad and Bruce came into the kitchen. "Hey, what's going on?" Dad asked us.

"Nothing!" I replied.

"Is he giving you trouble, Shelly?" Bruce started to say, but I cut him off.

"No! Eddie's fine," I said as I stomped back into the dining area with the guys following closely behind. Lisa was sitting in one of the booths with Robin and Roger who had just arrived. "We were just discussing something!"

"What?" Dad asked.

"Tell him, Shelly," Eddie said gently.

I let out an annoyed sigh. "I accidentally unleashed a destructive book demon, and I have no idea how to get rid of it!" I nearly yelled. This announcement made everyone, except Eddie, look at me as if I had gone completely stark, raving mad. Which, at this point, I was starting to feel like I had.

"You unleashed a demon?" Dad asked me. He had dealt with some nasty demons when he first bought this place, and believe you me, if it hadn't been for some of the locals here, he wouldn't be alive today. He didn't want to relive that chaotic time ever again. "You know how dangerous they are, Shelly!" he reprimanded me.

"Actually, this demon is different from the ones you dealt with, Mr. Anderson." Eddie explained. "It's more of a Level One demon than those Level Five demons. It's not so much dangerous as it is destructive." Wrong thing to say, Eddie.

"You put Shelly up to this, didn't you?" Bruce accused Eddie. He grabbed the vampire by the collar of his coat and was about to slam him up against one of the tables when Eddie turned himself into mist and slipped out of Bruce's grip. As angry as Bruce was, I couldn't have anticipated the surge of electricity that erupted from his hands without warning.

"What the?" Eddie shouted as he materialized again and leaped out of the way of the electricity.

Bruce looked at his hands in shock. "What just happened?" he asked, turning to my dad.

"Bruce," Dad said yanking his friend back away from Eddie, "if electricity is your magical ability—which I think it is—I certainly don't want you using it to attack someone! Is that clear?" He stared at Bruce with anger in his eyes.

Eddie was about to warn Bruce not to threaten him again when we heard a loud crash above us. I covered my head as huge pieces of wood and shards of light bulbs rained upon us. Looking up, I saw a long, spindly, hairy leg come right through the huge hole in the ceiling. The demon was Hell-bent on destroying the diner. I stood for a moment, paralyzed with fear. Then for the second time in two nights, Eddie saved me from the demon. He shoved me onto the floor as he shouted out another spell, "Citadel!" A pale green force field suddenly encircled me and the vampire.

I had never seen Eddie pull off this spell. So I was infatuated with the pretty color and hardly noticed my boyfriend pushing me toward the counter.

"Get behind the counter and stay there!" he ordered me as we crawled toward the destination. Once we were behind the safety of the counter, Eddie dropped the spell and went back out to help ward off the demon.

"Lisa," I ordered, "get over here!"

She scrambled behind the counter, and we watched the men battle the spider thing. Dad had a rifle in his hands and was shooting off a couple rounds. Bruce was shouting something as he stood there looking like a fool. Roger, who didn't want to injure his hip anymore, crawled under a table for protection. Robin was trying to summon the trees outside the diner to beat the spider to death. Even Eddie wasn't doing such a great job throwing his fireball spells. The whole place was getting more and more torn up by the demon.

I had to do something. From my position behind the counter, I spotted a vaporizer. The blue and silver guns look like they are from the set of a sci-fi movie. Cheesy and toy-like, they are extremely deadly weapons. They have three settings: Stun, Kill, and Vaporize. Each setting sends a certain amount of electrified energy. I grabbed the gun and slid the red lever to Kill. Aiming the gun, I peered over the top of the counter and fired. Blue bolts of energy hit the demon squarely between the eyes. The creature stopped for a moment and then went back to tearing up the diner. I threw the gun down in frustration. Crap! Nothing happened. It was as if someone blew a puff of air at the demon.

Then I remembered something Mr. Wolfbane told me: The demon grew around colored light. Maybe it would leave if there was no light. I raced towards the light switch and cast the entire building in complete darkness.

"Who killed the lights?" Robin yelled.

"I did!" I shouted. "Nobody move!" My command was heeded. I, along with everyone else, listened for a few breathless moments for the sound of cracking structure beams. The one thing that could be heard was the tick tock of the clock hanging directly above me. It's amazing how loud something can be when you're in complete darkness and silence. We all waited for another few more agonizing minutes. I wished I could know if the demon was still around. Then I decided to play on a hunch. *Eddie*, I asked subliminally, *can you sense the thermal heat of the demon?*

Yes! Want me to check it out if it is still hanging around? The vampire returned the message.

Please, and be careful.

Even though I couldn't see my hands in front of my face, I read Eddie's thoughts. He jumped high to one of the rafters, and then changed himself into mist as he floated up through the hole in the ceiling. A few minutes later, he came back down through the hole and materialized next to me. He laid a hand on my shoulder, making me jump. "It's gone!"

I flicked on the light. "Holy mess, Batman!" I said, amazed at the mess in the middle of the diner.

Once everyone had decided they were all right, Dad put his hands to the side of his head in frustration. "Oh, man! Oh, man! Oh, man!" he moaned. "This is going to take forever to clean up!"

Roger came out from his hiding place under the table. He grabbed his cane and was staring intently at the pile of debris in front of him. Suddenly, the pile gathered itself up and rushed at top speed towards the ceiling. Roger's gaze followed the moving pile as it reconstructed itself perfectly as though the demon had never attacked. We all stood in shock looking at Roger. Everyone that is, except for Eddie, who knew exactly what was going on with my friend.

"Rog, that was awesome!" Robin replied.

"Molecukinesis," the vampire murmured as he crossed his arms. "Great ability, Roger!"

"How do you know so much about magic?" Roger asked him.

Eddie shrugged. "I've been around a long time," he said.

Bruce's eyes narrowed at him. "I'll bet. You're just a nice vampire who thinks that he knows everything about this freaking weird place," he spat as he moved toward Eddie again.

"Bruce!" Robin moved him at the same time.

Bruce whirled around to face my father. "Timothy, why are you defending this thing? He's trouble, you know that! He tried to hurt Shelly with that green thing of his."

"Dad," Lisa said quietly, "Eddie's seems all right. He and his brother let us stay at their house last night after—." Her voice slowly trailed off as she realized that we were all staring at her in shock.

"You forced my daughter to stay in your castle?" Bruce demanded of Eddie.

Eddie's voice became low and dangerous. "I didn't force Lisa to do anything. And for your information, Mr. Miller, I would never ever hurt Shelly, or force her into any kind of situation that she would feel uncomfortable. I will protect her at any cost. And you know that too, Mr. Anderson."

"No!" I shouted. "There was a little incident at my house, and Eddie came to get us and said that we could stay at his place until my window is replaced."

"Your window?" Dad asked. He seemed more concerned that my window was damaged than the fact I had stayed at Eddie and Dirk's last night. "What happened to it?"

"The spider kind of took it out!" I said.

"Your landlord's going to blow a gasket," Robin said.

"Yeah, that's the least of my problems," I answered.

"How bad?" Dad asked.

"The entire window."

"Dad, don't worry. Rog and I put some plywood over it today," Robin said. Bruce was giving him a look that almost read you-knew-about-this-but did-nothing-to-stop-it. "Eddie's a great guy. I don't know what your problem is with him, Bruce." My brother was the type of guy who would stand by his friends through thick and thin.

"While your so-called boyfriend stood by and did nothing?" Bruce asked me. "Shelly, why are you trying to protect this creep?"

That did it. "Will you quit acting like two-year-olds, all of you!" I shouted. "There is a giant book demon roaming around town, and all you can do is fight! This is ridiculous! Bruce, you don't know Eddie like I do, and already you've made your bigoted decision about him! Dad, will you just forget all about the grudge you still hold against Bruce? And Eddie, I know you don't like Bruce! Will you at least try to be nice to him?"

"What have I done, Shelly?" Robin asked me.

"Shut up!" I snapped at my brother. I threw up my hands. "Grow up, all of you! We've got this freaking demon that I can't even stop!" I stopped in mid-rant as everyone looked absolutely shocked at the normally optimistic Shelly. I turned on my heel and ran out the back door.

I stepped onto the parking lot of the restaurant as a cool summer night breeze swept past me. Slamming the metal door behind me, I retreated to the edge of the lot and sank to the pavement. Sobs gushed out of me like Niagara Falls. This was all my fault, and I knew it. I didn't mean to unleash this beast, and now it was going to destroy the life that my family had made here in Zephyr. "Why does everyone expect me to stop it when I don't know the first thing about book demons?" And what about that stupid wish I made? Did I ask for Bruce to be such a jerk? All I wanted was to see my best friend from home again, and what did I get? Everyone angry at each other, and now at me because I just made such a good impression! To top it off, I wasn't even sure if my winged horse was still alive. "I hate this!" I screamed at the night.

"Shelly?" Eddie asked as he sat down beside me. He pulled me close to him as I continued crying on his shoulder. "Hey, shush, shush, it's all right!" he said, trying to get me to calm down. Like most guys, the vampire had no idea what to do when a girl is crying hysterically.

"No, it's not, Eddie," I said quietly as I managed to control my sobbing. "You expect me to know how to get rid of this dumb thing, but you forget that I haven't lived in Zephyr all my life. I'm sorry that I haven't read the latest edition of *Book Demons for Dummies*. I can't do this by myself!"

Eddie took out a bunch of napkins he had stuffed in his pants pocket earlier and wiped away some of the tears from my face. "Why didn't you tell me how you felt? I would've understood completely."

I was about to say he should have known, but then I remembered. I was the only telepath around here. "I'm sorry, Eddie. I thought you knew."

"Apology accepted. I'm not mad at you, but I think you should apologize to everyone downstairs. You were pretty harsh."

"I shouldn't have yelled at you. I'm just fed up with everything," I said quietly as I leaned my head against his shoulder.

"I know. Will it make you feel better if I did what you yelled at me for?"

I looked at him curiously. "What do you mean?"

"I'll try to be nice to Mr. Miller, even if he is a jerk."

I managed a smile. He would try, just for me. "Thanks!" I drew my knees close to my chest. "What about the spider thing?"

The vampire rubbed his chin in thought. "Well," he said after a few moments, "let's go to your house and grab that book. Then you and I will figure it out from there. Okay?"

I nodded. He helped me to my feet, and we walked back inside together.My arm slipped around his waist. He turned and smiled at me, indicating that he liked the physical touch between us. Nobody had moved much. "Dad, Eddie and I need to go back to my house to get the book that demon came out of."

"Do you think it's safe out there?" Dad asked us.

"We'll be okay, Mr. Anderson," Eddie assured as he put an arm around me. "We'll take my motorcycle. Don't worry. I won't let anything happen to her."

My father nodded. "I know you won't, Eddie."

Chapter Ten:
Why Tragedy Songs Aren't Good Choices for Karaoke

The ride home was uneventful. We didn't see the demon.

I raced inside and grabbed the book off my bookshelf. I placed

the book in the little box on the back of the motorcycle. Clipping

my helmet back on, I climbed back on the bike. Eddie revved up

the engine and we sped back towards the diner. I thought about

what little we had accomplished. We had the book, but how were

we going to get the demon back in the book when the thing was

about the size of Texas? I had told Eddie about the colored light

affect on this certain demon, but still we had no idea what to do

next.

I was pondering this as we were coming up to McAlly's

Tavern. I gave a small gasp the second I noticed the demon

advancing towards the bar. Eddie had also seen it and slowed down the motorcycle to an almost stop. He kept his hand on the gas in case the demon saw us and decided to play a deadly game of Duck, Duck, Goose. Suddenly, we heard one of the drunks inside belting out a horrific karaoke version of "You Sexy Thing."

The vampire and I watched in amazement as the demon spider stopped in its tracks the minute the music had started.

If you have ever heard a demon's scream, you will never forget it. The only way I can describe it is a cross between an extremely loud scraping fingernails across a blackboard and the whimpering noise a dying, injured animal makes. Unfortunately the helmet is not sound-proof, so I had to clamp my hands over my ears as the demon ran away screaming and shrinking. Shrinking? I had to blink again to make sure my eyesight wasn't failing. It was getting smaller, but how? Then I heard the awful music. So, that was it! I tapped Eddie on the shoulder. "The karaoke music is causing it to get smaller!" I almost shouted.

Eddie turned to congratulate me for figuring it all out when we both saw the spider heading towards us. *Hang on to me!* The vampire ordered me telepathically. I wrapped my arms around his waist as he gunned the engine. *I'm going to try to shake the demon off our tail*, he told me. The motorcycle gave a left turn so sharp that I almost felt the heat rise off the pavement. Well, I realized, this wasn't the first time I was riding a motorcycle and being chased by evil creatures.

We drove for about fifteen minutes along a fairly dark-side road. I kept looking over my shoulder. The thing was still following us. What was Eddie doing? Then once I read his mind, I realized he was luring the demon away from the colored lights so that it wouldn't grow anymore. Finally I noticed we were on some very bumpy grass. Eddie killed both the headlight and the engine the minute we were under a cluster of trees. I obeyed the vampire's subliminal order not to make a sound. I began to formulate an idea on how to get rid of the demon as we heard it tromping blindly through the woods. I took out my cell phone and quietly sent text messages to Strider and Robin, asking both of them to bring the infamous karaoke machine and Robin's band amplifiers to the diner.

What are you doing, Shelly?

I have a great idea to get rid of the demon. But I need to ask Strider and Robin to bring some things to my dad's place. I'll tell you about it when we get back, Eddie, but right now you're going to have to trust me on this one.

Eddie didn't say anything, but I knew he did trust me, no matter how crazy my plan sounded. Finally, he started up the engine and sped back to the diner in a record time of five minutes. I swear we ran more red lights on the way back than when we were running away from the demon.

Strider was talking with Robin and Roger when we arrived back at the restaurant. The satyr looked up at me with irritation. "Two questions, Shelly: Number one, why is Jordan over at my place?"

I was taken aback. "What do you mean? Is she all right?"

Strider shrugged. "I don't know. I've been out of town for a few days, and when I got back, I found her pacing around in

Longfellow's stable. She seems to be alright." Longfellow happened to be the winged horse that sired Jordan. I was impressed and touched at the same time. My winged horse had flown to her father for protection.

I glanced over at Eddie who was smiling at me. He was thinking about it, but he might have well said, "See, I told you she was going to be alright."

"Question number two: Why did you ask me to bring my karaoke machine?" Strider's question brought me back to the subject at hand. "Because I highly doubt Mr. Anderson has reconsidered his veto."

"Look, you know about the giant spider that has been destroying the town?"

The satyr nodded. "So what?" he asked.

"It's actually a book demon that I accidentally unleashed." The horrified look on Strider's face was priceless. I decided to lessen the shock by explaining to him my fool-proof plan. Or, should I say, foolish plan? "Well, I've come up with a plan to stop it!" That stopped everyone's conversations as they turned towards me. "When Eddie and I went to get the book the demon came from, we saw the spider thing heading towards McAlly's Tavern."

"So, he wanted a drink," Robin commented with a shrug.

I chose to ignore my brother. "Apparently it was karaoke night at the bar, and when the music came on, the demon started shrinking. So, I had this plan to use Strider's karaoke machine and the band's amplifiers at the stand in the park-you know, the one they use for summer concerts—to make the demon shrink back to its normal size."

Dad held up his hands. "Whoa, whoa, whoa, Shelly! I'm sorry, but your plan is just not going to work." He wasn't trying to belittle me. He was just being logical.

"And in case this does work," Bruce pointed out, "how are you going to get the demon to cooperate?"

I glanced over at Eddie for support. He had been listening to my plan and mulling it over in his mind at the same time. Finally, he stepped into the conversation with an idea. "I've got an answer for that, Mr. Miller. Shelly told me that the demon is attracted to colored lights. If she wants to, Lisa can lure the demon to the park with her photokinesis."

"What!" the Millers all said at the same time.

"You're not putting my daughter's life in danger!" Bruce snapped. "You've done enough of that with Shelly."

"I said 'if she wants to,'" the vampire corrected as he tried to keep his temper under control.

Roger spoke up. "Dad, if Lisa agrees to this, I'll go with her. We can ride on Robin's dragon. I've gotten pretty good at controlling Cornelius."

Lisa threw her hands up. Apparently, she felt out of place. "Since everyone wants me to be a part of this crazy idea, I'll do it." She glared at Eddie, no doubt, for attempting to send her on a death sentence.

About an hour later, Eddie was jumping off the little stage with the white gazebo covering which was set up right smack dab in the middle of Zephyr Center Park. He had just finished helping Strider and Robin set up the karaoke machine and the amps. He came over by my side, noticing the nervous look in my eyes. "You okay, Shelly?" he asked.

I got up from my knees where I had just finished laying out the book on the damp grass. "No, I'm scared," I admitted in a soft whisper.

"Don't worry," my boyfriend replied as he gave me a reassuring hug. "I'll be right up on the stage with you." He gave me a kiss on the top of my head.

As I wrapped my arms around him, I wanted him to hold me until this nightmare was all over. "What if the thing attacks us?"

"Then I'll use my force field spell to protect us."

I looked up at him. "Was that the thing you did earlier tonight with the green force thingy?"

Eddie nodded.

We heard a sudden cough behind us and we both saw Dad standing there. "Okay, you two lovebirds."

The vampire and I immediately backed away from each other as I covered up my cheeks with my hands to stop the sudden onset of embarrassment. "So, Dad," I smiled nervously, "did Bruce finally agree to power the machine with his electricity?"

Dad nodded. "Reluctantly."

"I heard that, Timothy," Bruce said with a forced smile as he came from the back of the stage. He jammed his hands into the side pockets of the jeans he borrowed from my dad. "You think this is going to work?" The question was directed at Dad, but I answered anyway.

"I hope so." I began making little geometric shapes in the grass with the toe of my right sneaker. It had been only ten minutes since Lisa and Roger took off on Robin's dragon, but for some unknown reason, I was getting really worried.

"Yo, Shelly, Eddie!" Strider called from backstage. "We're all set up!" He tossed us two microphones. "Your first song is 'Teen Angel.'"

Eddie and I looked at him dubiously. "The song about the teen who gets hit by a train, Strider?"

"You said to grab one of my karaoke CDs! You didn't specify which one you wanted." the satyr said as he jumped off the stage. "I handpicked all of these songs."

"In what dimension, does an epic tragedy song qualify as a great karaoke song?" I asked.

"Shelly," Eddie reminded me, "this is karaoke music we're talking about. It doesn't have to make sense."

I read the back of the CD case. "'Tin Man'? 'Macarthur Park'? 'Run, Joey, Run'? 'Poor, Poor Pitiful Me.' 'Billy, Don't Be A Hero.' 'Wildfire.' Good God, Strider, these songs are just depressing."

"It was this or polka music. Just read the words on the screen, and you guys will be fine."

I glanced over at the vaporizer which I had brought with me. Maybe after we got rid of the demon, I would use the gun on the satyr. "Fine!"

"Ready, Shelly?" Eddie asked me. He pointed to the sky as Robin's green and black dragon came into view. He leaped on the stage just as the demon came into the park clearing.

I inhaled a huge breath and climbed on the stage with Eddie. Lisa finally killed her colored lights just as Roger directed Cornelius to go behind the stage. Dad and Bruce disappeared out back as well. Bruce must have started up his electric power because a bolt of lightning flashed behind the gazebo.

Finally, we heard the music start. I glanced over at the machine looking for Robin or Strider, but they weren't anywhere in sight. That meant the CD in the player was running by itself. Great, who knew what songs were coming up next.

"Teen angel, teen angel, teen angel, ooh, ooh!" My voice quavered a bit as I started to sing along. *Please, start shrinking! I don't know how long I can take singing this depressing song.* I pleaded silently with the demon.

Glancing over at my boyfriend, I saw him make a gun with his free hand and pretend to shoot himself with it. He joined me. "That fateful night the car was stalled upon the railroad track. I pulled you out, and we were safe, but you went running back." Who in their right mind thought that this was a great song?

Surprisingly, our joyless song must have worked because the demon started getting smaller. After a few seconds, the thing had shrunk from Godzilla-size to elephant-size. Then I sank to my knees as I remembered and heard the awful screaming. My microphone dropped to the stage as I placed my hands over my ear to muffle the sound.

Shelly, Eddie's telepathic message came like an arrow on my mind, *get up and sing!* The machine had gone to the next song which happened to be the worst song of all time: MacArthur Park. If the shrieking was bothering the vampire (I didn't have the time or the energy to try to read his mind), he was hiding it quite well. He bent down beside me and grabbed my hand.

I can't! The screaming hurts my ears! Even though the screams blasted my eardrums, I pulled myself up with Eddie's help and joined in the singing.

When we got to the chorus, all hell broke loose. Eddie and I sang, "Someone left the cake out in the rain. I don't think that I can take it 'cause it took so long to bake it and I'll never have that recipe again. Oh, nooo!" The spider took a swing at us with one of its massive, spindly legs.

Eddie let go of his microphone. "Get down!" We both dropped to the ground as the leg sent the karaoke box careening off the stage and crashing to the ground. "Wow!" Eddie said. "Even demons can't stand that song."

"Crap!" I said, realizing that my plan had failed. The second I spotted the vaporizer, my brain stopped thinking logically. I scrambled to my feet and grabbed the vaporizer. "Let's see if ten thousand volts of electrified energy will stop you," I told the book demon as I placed the gun in Vaporize mode. I leaped off the stage and ran under the spider.

I knelt down on the grass and hoisted the gun to my shoulder. "Eat volts!" I shouted as I pulled the trigger.

White hot bolts of electricity shot out from the barrel and hit the spider's underbelly at full force. The creature staggered back in a daze, but I didn't wait for it to recover. "This is for my bedroom window!" I yelled as I pulled the trigger again. This time, the shot hit the spider at full force in the face and blew a hole in the abdomen. I fired a third and final time. Moments later there was a loud BOOM!

Eddie ran up to me and held me close as he shouted "Citadel!" The green force field protected us from pieces of flying book demon. He glanced at me with a fanged smile as he let down the force field. "Nice shooting there, Tex," he said as he disarmed me and set the gun down on the ground.

"Where did it go?" I asked, breathing heavily.

"Here, there, everywhere. I'm never going to get on your bad side."

I breathed a huge sigh of relief. "I did it, Eddie!" I said. "I got rid of the book demon."

"Yep, I don't think it's coming back anytime soon. That was some awesome shooting!"

Then I did something unexpected. I kissed the vampire on the lips. Eddie didn't object and returned my kiss. A few minutes passed before I could pull myself away from him. I was blushing big time, but I didn't care. I had defeated the demon so I kissed my boyfriend.

Eddie glanced down at the book lying on the grass. "What should we do with your book?"

"Normally, I don't advocate destroying a book, being a librarian and all," I said, "but this time I'm going to make an exception. Torch it!"

Everything went back to normal the next few days. Roger was a big help in reconstructing the destroyed property by his molecukinesis. Dad hired Bruce on as the diner's new cook. I got a new bedroom door, a new window, and Lisa became my new roommate.

I was telling Eddie all this one night as we were browsing around in a bookstore. He had picked up a book about natural disasters. "Look what I found, Shelly!" He flipped through the pages. A fanged grin spread across his face. "And, what do you know? It's demon-free!"

"Shut up!"

COMING SOON

Secrets of the Undead

My Life Among the Undead: Book 3

Everyone has secrets, including Shelly Anderson's vampire boyfriend, Eddie Van Helsing. When Shelly accepts a temporary job as a librarian at the Urbana College of Magic, an Ivy League school for wizards and enchantresses, Eddie doesn't want her to go. When she asks him why he refuses to give her any information and purposely blocks her mind-reading attempts. At the college, Shelly discovers a strange connection to Eddie's past and a forty-year-old murder. She must solve this mystery on her own with a ghost who refuses to talk to her, a creepy professor with a shady past, and a quirky roommate with a tendency to snoop. What is the college hiding from Shelly? How is Eddie connected to everything?

About the Author

Camara Bragdon has her master's degree in library and information science and lives in Maine. This is the second book in her vampire series, *My Life among the Undead*.

www.ingramcontent.com/pod-product-compliance
Lightning Source LLC
Chambersburg PA
CBHW060414310726
48976CB00003B/1043